TROUBLE IN DISGUISE

Trouble In Love Series

SONIA STANIZZO

Trouble in Disguise

Copyright © 2019, 2022 Sonia Stanizzo

First Published by: Beachwalk Press, Inc 2019

Second Edition: 2022

ISBN: 978-0-6450908-8-8 (ebook)

ISBN: 978-0-645-0908-9-5 (print)

Publisher: JRL Publishing

Cover Design: Outlined with Love Designs

To my husband Tom. You make me believe I can do anything.

Chapter 1

*J*ade Brennan screeched with horror as she stared at her disheveled reflection. She groaned as she stood in front of the public restroom's mirror at Brimland Point Arena.

"Oh God, this is worse than I thought." She yanked paper towels from the metal dispenser on the wall. "No wonder the security guard only invited you backstage and screwed his nose up at me," she called out to her cousin Liz, who was in one of the cubicles.

"It's not that bad," Liz yelled back.

"Pfft, it's worse. I showed up at the concert looking cute. The clock ticked midnight and now I resemble roadkill."

Something dark and sticky was smeared on her black and red polka-dot shirt. She didn't want to know what it could be. And her white jeans had what she hoped was only beer stains splattered down her right leg. Being pressed up against sweaty bodies while they headbanged to heavy rock music was hazardous.

Jade dampened the paper towel and scrubbed away the smudged mascara from under her eyes. "Waterproof my arse. And let's not get me started on what's happened to my hair."

Her difficult-to-manage red curls had escaped from the ponytail and now lay tangled and knotted around her face. The humidity in the arena was doing a great job of making her look like she'd just stepped out of a pressure cooker.

The toilet flushed, and Liz walked to the sink and washed her hands. Her lips twitched as she took in Jade's appearance. It was so great to see her cousin smile again. After Liz's fiancé dumped her at the altar on their wedding day, she'd been a blubbering mess. It had taken Jade three months to get her out of the house.

But Liz should have seen the break-up coming. With their family history she should have known it wouldn't work. When would the Brennan women learn to never fall in love? The men in their lives always left.

A tug pulled at Jade's heart. Never having someone to love was depressing, but over the years she'd learned to live with it. It was better not to find love at all. It only left you with a broken heart. She'd seen it too many times.

"Oh my God, freaking Harvey's Territory wants us backstage." Liz broke into a huge smile, and her eyes sparkled.

"No, the giant security guard said they wanted *you*, not me. I look like a hot mess, and you just look hot. I'm only the tag-along who insisted I join you. Why did you have to flash the lead singer your boobs?"

Liz laughed. "I've had too much to drink, and you know how I act when I get tipsy. Anyway, it got us *backstage!*"

Yeah, when Liz was drinking, she liked to perform stripteases, no matter where she was, and that was why Jade insisted on going backstage too. Who knew the trouble Liz might find? Jade didn't want a random guy taking advantage of her cousin.

"And did you see him smile when I did? God, he's so sexy." Liz fanned her face. "I hope I get to talk to him or..." She smirked.

Jade had noticed he was kind of cute if you liked that long-haired, tattooed, grungy look. And when he smiled his lips tilted in a crooked way that *was* sexy. Liz would definitely be easy prey.

"Maybe we should go home," Jade suggested.

"No way! We'll never have this opportunity again. It will be fun. I think I deserve it after the hell I've been through." The sparkle dimmed from her eyes, and Jade didn't want to see her miserable again.

"Okay, but if they want us to join in some twisted, kinky orgy, we're leaving."

"You won't regret it, I promise." Liz pulled her into a hug. "Hurry and fix yourself, I can't wait to meet them." She bounced around like an excited toddler waiting to meet Santa.

With a pinched expression, Jade examined her

makeup. "Go ahead, and I'll catch up. It'll take a few minutes to clean this mess."

"Are you sure?"

"Yes. I'll see you soon."

Liz squealed and raced out of the room.

Once Jade did all she could to improve her appearance, she left the bathroom. The huge, beefy security guard with no neck had given them directions to the party when he'd been called to attend a problem and couldn't escort them himself. She found the corporate area above the arena, but it was a labyrinth of corridors and rooms.

Did Mountain Man say left or right at the end of this corridor? She should have paid more attention. She took a guess and turned right, walked down another corridor, and found the double timber doors he'd mentioned. "Which one did he say to take?"

She pressed an ear against each of them. Shouldn't there be music pounding through them to indicate the right one? But she heard nothing.

To decide which one to take, she pointed her finger and sang, "Eeny, meeny, miny, moe. Door on the right it is." And she pushed through.

It was another hallway with offices lining each side. She glanced back over her shoulder. If she continued, would she remember the way out? Deciding she wouldn't go too far, just in case, she peered through the windows, finding them empty.

"This can't be where the party is." As she turned to go back, she came across a room with the blinds pulled down, covering the windows, but she still didn't hear any music. "Maybe it's one of those soundproof rooms," she said as she opened the door and stepped inside the dim space.

Immediately, she knew she was in the wrong place. There was no raging party. In fact, it was another empty room.

"I shouldn't have eaten my packet of chips. I could have used them as a trail to find my way out of this maze. Now I'll get so lost I'll never find my way out, and then someone will find my bones in an old janitor's cupboard," she mumbled as she turned to leave.

"Is there room in that cupboard for two?"

With a gasp, Jade spun around and came face-to-face with trouble.

———

Nathan Harvey dropped heavily onto an old, leather lounge in a dark office he'd stumbled into. Far enough away from the party his band was having. He blew out a long breath and scrubbed his hands over his face. Why after every show did they need to party like they were still twenty-one-year-old kids? For Nathan, the shine had worn off years ago.

In fact, he never liked the backstage scene. It wasn't like he could get involved in the party. He didn't drink excessively or do drugs, not that he allowed anything illegal at them, and he couldn't get close to anyone they invited to join them in case they discovered his secret.

Eventually he learned it was easier to hide in an empty room to get away from it all. But lately not even playing music—what he loved to do most in the world—was worth the isolation. Touring became a lonely gig.

With jerky movements, he shrugged off his leather jacket and threw it on the floor. How much longer could he keep going, pretending to be someone else?

Music is in your blood, just like it's in mine. Promise me you'll never let it die. Whenever the urge to quit clouded his thoughts, his father's words blew them away.

Tonight was the last show for their Australian leg of the tour and the start of a much-needed break in his hometown for a few weeks before they headed to Europe and played more sold-out shows. Nathan often wondered if his dad could see how far he'd come, would he be proud? He'd never know. But deep down, he hoped so, because he was the reason Nathan played in a heavy rock band. Did that little boy who once yearned for his father's approval think he'd get it now in some freakish spiritual way?

A noise from across the office stopped his musings, and a petite redhead stumbled into the room. Man, how did these women find him? He made sure no one spotted him leaving the party.

He was about to ask her to leave when she mumbled something about chips and a janitor's cupboard, and instead of getting rid of her, he rose from the chair and asked if there was room in that cupboard for two. Because for a moment hiding away with a cute redhead sounded more appealing than being alone.

The light shining from the hallway into the open doorway showed curls from a messy hairstyle bouncing around a creamy, smooth face clear of makeup. She had sparkling blue eyes, and a dusting of freckles spread along her nose and cheeks. Not the typical groupie with skin-tight clothing and a made-up face. He liked the simplicity of this woman, and he couldn't deny she was cute, but a groupie was a groupie, and Nathan didn't indulge in them. So why did looking at her blast a surge of heat through his body?

"It's you...the singer guy." Her eyes grew wide, and her breath got a little choppy.

And suddenly, the heat disappeared, and a chill blanketed over him. There were different types of groupies. The ones who acted surprised when they *accidentally* ran into him. And the ones who brazenly told him exactly what they wanted to do with him. She fell into the first category.

"Don't act so shocked you found me. I should have known I couldn't sneak out undetected." He turned away to dismiss her.

"Found you? No, I was looking for the party—"

He swung back around. "Look, Freckles." She gasped at the reference and covered her nose with her hand. "No offense, but I'm not into groupies. If you go back to the party, I'm sure Mike or Chris will be happy to take you on."

The hand covering her nose dropped, and she frowned. "*Take me on?* You think I want... I want..."

Some women tried to deny it, but they were always

after the same thing. A hook-up with a band member. "If you go back down the hall and take the other timber door, you'll find the party."

Her posture stiffened, and she puffed out her chest. It wasn't *Playboy* magazine worthy, but with it heaving like she'd run a marathon, it drew his attention, and the heat worked its way back.

"For your information, Mr. Grunge Band on Steroids, I got separated from my cousin, and I'm trying to find her. I'm *not* a groupie looking for who knows what with Mike or Chris, nor am I interested in you. *And* I spend a lot of money on creams to lighten my freckles, so how dare you point them out!"

Nathan let out a surprised bark of laughter. This woman was as fiery as her red hair. He ambled closer to the little spitfire. She'd caught his attention, and if she meant what she said, he'd have no chance getting anything from her. Time for the test.

"I happen to think your freckles are sexy." When he took another step closer, her cheeks flushed pink and she sucked in a breath. He fingered a loose curl on her neck, making sure he touched the exposed skin. "Maybe I won't send you to Mike or Chris. I've never had a hot redhead before." He cupped her face and pretended to lean in as if to kiss her. She'd soon show her true colors.

But instead of her claiming his kiss, one of her hands slammed a palm onto his forehead and the other wrapped around the wrist touching her hair. "What the hell are you doing?"

For a moment he was stunned. This woman who was

small enough to fit in his pocket held him back like she was double his size. "Honey, you're playing the *shy fan* a little too seriously."

"I told you, I'm not here for any groupie gangbang. I'm looking for my cousin!" she said, and flung her hand away from his head. Some strands of hair got caught in a ring on her finger, and the wig he was wearing went flying from his head and hung from her hand like a dead, black cat.

With wide eyes, the woman looked from her hand to his head and back down to the wig. "Ummm, I think this belongs to you?"

Slowly, she held it out, and he snatched it from her grasp. It was still tangled around her fingers, and the force made her stumble into his chest. She clasped his arms to steady herself. After a beat she rubbed her hands along his arms. Not in a flirty, trying to feel him up kind of way. More like trying to figure out why he felt like stocking mesh instead of smooth skin.

Nathan stepped back, held her hand, and untangled the wig from her fingers. *Fuck!* He never let anyone outside of the band and family get close enough to stumble upon his secret. Now this redhead would ruin everything; his band and identity would be destroyed.

Dammit. Why did he have to get so close? Test or no test, she was one hot firecracker and he couldn't help himself. Now, after a moment of stupidity, years of keeping his identity a secret was flying out the window.

Turning his back on her, he threw the wig on the

lounge, clenched his fists, and took a deep breath. "Forget what you saw here."

"But…why—"

"If you breathe a word to anyone, I'll sue your arse off." He swung around, his muscles quivering. "Understood?"

She quickly nodded.

At her startled expression, he deflated. "Get out," he said as he turned his back on her again.

The sound of the door closing echoed through the room.

Chapter 2

"What the hell just happened?" Jade mumbled as she scuttled down the corridor.

The long-haired, lead singer of Harvey's Territory with the silver nose ring, black studs up his left ear, and black, messy hair wasn't the grungy rock star the world saw. Underneath the black wig was dark, sandy-colored hair, which even though flattened, looked neatly cut, short around the sides with a little longer tussle on top. Without the long locks covering his face, and even with his angry expression, he was hot. Why would he want to hide such good looks?

Rounding the end of the corridor, Jade bumped into a tall, solid wall and stumbled a couple of steps back. A hand reached out, stopping her from falling. The security guard that led them backstage scowled at her.

"Why the hell are you wandering around?" he demanded as he searched the corridor behind her.

"Sorry, I got lost."

He lifted a skeptical eyebrow and grumbled, "*Lost…* that's what they all say. Anyway, your friend's been looking for you."

Jade huffed and slammed her hands on her hips. She was getting tired of people around here not believing her. "I did get lost. This place is like a freaking maze, and *your* instructions were stupid."

The guard's frown deepened, and he pointed a stumpy finger at her face. "Listen, lady, if I had a dollar for every skanky groupie that chased after Nathan and his boys, I'd be a rich fucking man. You're not the first chick to get *lost*, and you won't be the last. Now go find your friend or I'll kick your arse outta here."

Jade gasped, but before she could come up with a scathing comeback, a deep voice shot out behind her. "Trent, get the fuck out of here."

Turning around, Jade almost bumped into the lead singer, he was standing so close. The wig was back, and a black leather jacket with chains hanging from it covered the tattoos.

"Just as soon as I get rid of this skank for you," the security guard said.

Jade huffed at the insult.

"No need. You're fired," the singer said with deadly calm.

The guard's eyes bugged out of his head. "Come on, Nathan, you don't mean that. You told me you wanted no one sneaking around here, and she's some bimbo trying to get into your pants."

The singer, who she now knew was named Nathan, spoke with a tone more like a growl. "And you didn't do a great job of that either, did you? Now get the fuck out."

"But—"

"Now!"

The guard jumped. Even Jade flinched at the harshness of his voice. She watched as Trent hurried away.

"I'm sorry he spoke to you like that." Nathan's dark brown eyes looked at her with a gentle expression, and Jade was a little taken aback. Only moments ago he'd threatened to sue her, and now he'd defended her against a big, muscly security guard he'd nearly brought to tears. Could tonight get any weirder?

"It's okay. I could've taken him on. Mr. Gym-Junkie wasn't so scary. But did you have to fire him? Maybe he's got a family to provide for, or pets to feed. I bet he has rabbits. He looks like a rabbit kind of guy."

Nathan's lips twitched, then he flashed a white smile so hot it shot into her chest like a lightning bolt. The term *killer smile* was created for one like that, because for a second, she could have sworn her heart stopped beating.

"Rabbits?" He grinned, not realizing her chest problems might be critical and he would've had to give her CPR. Actually, those full lips on her mouth and his hands on her chest would be worth the cardiac arrest. God, where were these thoughts sprouting from?

"Okay, not rabbits, he'd probably eat them, but someone might depend on him," she said.

"Don't worry. I'll set him up someplace else so he can feed his…rabbits."

This time Nathan didn't hold back, and the smile turned into a laugh. The deep, husky sound sent a warm flush over her skin like she'd stepped too close to a fire. Moving away, she mentally shook herself. She needed to find Liz and get the hell out of there.

"Thanks for helping me out with Mr. Gym-Junkie, but I better find my cousin. She might get worried and call Brimland Police Department to report a homicide." She pointed in the direction they'd come from. "And what I saw back there…I promise not to say a word."

The smile that was still playing on his lips dropped into a flat line. The muscles tensed around his jaw, and his face looked hard as stone. "No one can know about that. I wasn't joking about suing you." His tone matched the cold expression on his face.

Wow, could this be a case of Dr. Jekyll and Mr. Hyde? "I don't need you to threaten me with a lawsuit to keep quiet."

"It wasn't a threat."

Trying not to explode, she inhaled deeply and mentally counted to five like she did when she was in a classroom of rowdy six-year-old children. "You're a jerk. You accuse me of stalking you like a horny groupie, you try to come onto me for who knows what reason, and then threaten me—no, not threaten, *warn* me you'll sue if I tell anyone your dirty little secret. Well, I'm sorry to break it to you, Mr. Rock Star, but I don't care who you are and have no interest in telling anyone about your Hannah Montana secret." With that, she spun on her heels and stormed away, the deep breathing and counting exercise failing miserably.

At the end of the corridor, instead of turning left—the direction she needed to take to get the hell out of there—she turned right and realized her mistake a second too late. She stopped, spun around, and with her head held high, continued past the corridor entrance where she'd left Nathan, and in her peripheral vision she saw him laughing. Probably at her terrible sense of direction. *Jerk.*

Chapter 3

Two nights later, Nathan Harvey sat in a booth at Jovi's Pub without his disguise. Nate Miller was the person he really was. The one that felt most comfortable—where he could breathe in peace without the attention and scrutiny of the public.

"Man, we spent many Saturday nights here when we were younger," Nate's childhood friend Toby said, sitting opposite him with a beer tilted to his lips. "Although, I was the one doing the drinking while you sang on that wooden stage to an uninterested crowd. How times have changed." He chuckled before taking a swig.

"They sure have," Nate agreed.

Now he grabbed the attention of thousands of people before he even opened his mouth. And as he looked at the small, empty spot where musicians came in the hope of the success Nate had achieved, he missed the simplicity.

"Happy to be back home?" Toby asked. "It's been what, two, three years?"

"Three, and yeah, I've missed the place."

"Just missed the place?" his friend said with a raised eyebrow.

Nate grinned, knowing what Toby was getting at. "Missed my grandmother too."

"Whatever," Toby grumbled, causing Nate to laugh.

"You know I missed you, mate. But you just flew out to see me two months ago."

"Big shot rock star didn't have much time for me," Toby mumbled into his bottle.

"God, you're sounding like a girlfriend. Maybe if I buy you something pretty it will make you happy?" Nate snickered.

"Whatever." Toby flipped him the bird. Then dropping all pretense, he said, "It must be nice to stop touring for a few weeks."

It felt like the weight of the world had been lifted from his shoulders. "Yeah, I needed a break."

"Can't be easy living in your disguise for so long without messing it up and revealing who you really are."

With a heavy sigh, Nate slouched in the seat. Toby was the only friend he trusted with the secret. And he'd kept it for over ten years. "I did mess it up."

"What?" Toby almost jumped out of his chair. "What the hell did you do?"

"I got too close to a groupie. Well, I thought she was one, but I'm not so sure what she was." When Toby stared at him wide-eyed with confusion, Nate continued. "Like I said, I got too close to this girl, and my wig got tangled in her fingers and it fell off."

Toby blew out a long breath, slouched over the table, and leaned closer to Nate, whispering, "This makes no sense. No one gets that close to you. How did this happen? I've seen nothing in the media about it. Shit..." He pulled out his phone from his jean's pocket and tapped at the screen. "Surely I would have seen something by now?"

"There's nothing there." Nate had already checked. For two days he'd checked on the hour, every hour. And he'd seen nothing.

"She's keeping quiet? I find that hard to believe. Do you realize how much money she'd make from exposing you?"

"I threatened to sue if she said anything. It must've worked."

"Man, if this were to get out, you'd never have peace again," Toby pointed out.

It was exhausting living a double life. The reason for the disguise was so he could have a normal one. Not fall into the rock star lifestyle that killed his parents. It was hard work but worth the anonymity. Still, sometimes he wondered if it would be so bad if he gave up the secret.

"I think I'm safe," Nate said.

Toby blew out a breath. "You must be slipping. You're never that careless."

A tiny redhead who had the temper of someone twice her size had distracted him, making him forget the rules he'd set in place. "Don't worry, I won't make that mistake again."

"For your sake, I hope you don't," Toby said as he

signaled to the waiter for another two beers. "Any plans while you're home?"

"Not much. I'll be spending time with my grandmother, help her around the house."

Toby laughed. "Fiona would spit fire at the suggestion. That woman has never needed help a day in her life. I've never seen anyone so independent."

"Or damn stubborn." His grandmother, the woman who raised him from the age of twelve, was the toughest yet most loving woman he'd ever known. But Toby was right, she'd have a fit if she knew he wanted to help. "Looks like I'm gonna have a lot of time on my hands."

The waiter arrived with their drinks and set them on the table. Sipping on his Corona, Toby looked at Nate intensely.

"Mate, first you're bitching that I'm not seeing you enough, now you're looking at me like I'm your next meal," Nate said. "I love ya, man, but I'm not on that side of the fence. Didn't think you were either."

"You'd be fucking lucky to have me."

Nate snickered, and Toby flipped him the bird again.

"I was thinking you might help me out while you're in town. I have a teacher at my primary school who's been on my back about wanting a music program for the kids. Parents have showed an interest in putting them in after-school lessons but can't afford them. And she wants to help."

"Doesn't the school have a program in their curriculum?"

"Yes, we do, but according to Jade, my teacher, she

wants the kids to learn more than tapping a triangle and clapping their hands to a beat. We don't have extra time during school hours, so she's planning on lessons after school for those kids who are interested."

"Sounds like a great idea. What is it you need me to do?"

Toby twisted the beer bottle in his hands. "I want you to teach the kids."

"You want me to teach *kids*?" His voice rose with surprise.

"Yep, and for free."

He loved the idea, but he wasn't the right guy for the job. "I have no idea how to teach kids. I'm not even sure I know how to teach music. I can play with my eyes closed, but helping someone else learn, especially children, is another story."

"Jade will always be there to help keep them in line. All you have to do is show them the basics. Teach them a simple song. We've got access to a few guitars, a keyboard, drums, and a few other instruments, but if you have anything we could borrow, it would help."

His grandmother's garage was filled with equipment he'd learned to play over the years.

"Surely you could find someone else?" he asked hopefully.

"At the moment we can't find anyone to do it for free, and we don't have the funds in our budget to pay someone. So, you've come home at a perfect time, *and* you're free." Toby smiled sweetly. It looked ridiculous on a grown arsed man.

"And if I say no?"

"Then you're an arsehole."

"When do I start?"

"Give me a couple of days to run things past Jade," Toby said.

Nate's stomach clenched. What the hell had he gotten himself into?

Chapter 4

*J*ade sat in the teacher staff room eating last night's spaghetti marinara, annoyed because a drop of red sauce had splashed onto her cream-colored blouse. Rubbing it with a napkin had only made it worse, and now it looked like she'd been stabbed in the heart.

Toby entered the room, and his gaze went straight to the crime scene. "You really need to keep spare clothes at work or wear a hazmat suit."

Crumpling her napkin, she aimed it at his head, but it didn't have enough force to hit its mark. He chuckled.

"What are you doing here anyway?" she asked. "I thought you had a meeting with the education department."

"They postponed it, so decided I'd have lunch with my favorite teacher." He pulled out a seat, sat next to her, and unwrapped his sandwich.

"Don't let Simone hear you say that. How many times

today has she needed you in her classroom to *help* with a problem?"

Toby sighed then ran a hand through his golden-brown hair which had a tenancy to fall over his forehead. "Twice."

"You need to tell her you're not interested."

Taking off his black-framed glasses, he put them on the table and rubbed his eyes. "I've tried, she's not listening. I don't want to talk about Simone, I've got good news for you."

Jade sat up straight in her chair. "You do?"

"Yes. I found a teacher for your music program."

Slapping her hands over her heart, she bounded off the chair. "That's fantastic, Toby. How did you manage it? I really thought we'd have so much trouble finding someone who'd do it for free."

"An old friend of mine, who's a music genius, is staying in town for a few weeks. But don't get too excited, once he leaves, we're going to have to find a replacement."

"That will give us time to work something out," she said as she paced the small room. "I need to get the hall ready, the instruments will need tuning, I'll send out a newsletter notifying families…" Dropping back in the seat, she placed her elbows on the table and plonked her chin in her hands. "This guy is awesome for doing this. I love him already. In fact, I'll give him my first-born child for doing such a wonderful thing for these kids. No one wants to give their time to us for nothing. I owe him a huge kiss. When do I get to meet him?"

Toby nodded in the direction of the door behind her. "Right now. Jade, meet Nate Miller."

A flush of heat crept up her neck and over her face. She wanted to slide under the table, but it was too late to hide and pretend the music teacher hadn't heard her. She turned slowly in the chair.

"Hello, Freckles." A smirk played on his lips.

Tilting her head to the side, her eyes narrowed as she took in the tall stranger with dark, sandy blond hair in Toby's office. But why had he called her Freckles? No one except the nasty singer from the concert called her... Wait...could it be?

She looked at the sexy, crooked grin on his face then gasped. "It's you!"

Toby eyed them both. "You know each other?"

"Yes," Nate answered.

"No," Jade responded.

"Hmm, that really clears things up."

"We've met—kind of—but we don't *know* each other," Jade explained.

Toby put his glasses back on and slid them up his nose, looking at Nate with a raised eyebrow like he was asking him for a better explanation.

"Remember what I told you the other night about the wig incident?"

Toby's mouth opened and closed, then he slapped the table and laughed. "Jade was the groupie you got too close to?"

"Hey! I'm not a damn groupie." She pointed a finger at Nate. "And will *never* be one, especially *yours*."

The smirk on Nate's lips grew into a huge smile, and once again a shot of electricity hit her chest. Did she need to start carrying around a portable defibrillator now that they would be working together?

Working together! How could she work with him? He was rude, and his moods changed quicker than her underwear.

"Why would a big rock star want to waste his time teaching a bunch of kids music? You must have better things to do with your time like…sex, drugs, and rock-and-roll."

Jade couldn't believe how effective Nate's disguise was as her gaze traveled over him. If he hadn't called her Freckles, she never would have guessed even though she'd seen him without the wig.

He crossed his arms over his chest. She couldn't help noticing the lean, toned muscles defined under his dark blue t-shirt, and her belly did a little flip-flop. And his smile, along with his good mood, dropped.

"I've put that on hold for a few weeks."

She averted her gaze, feeling a stab of guilt for hitting what must be a sore spot, then focused her attention on Toby, whose shoulders were shaking from laughter. "Do you find this situation amusing? He threatened to sue my arse off, and you want him around our young kids?" She was judging Nate's character before she got to know him, but hey, he'd judged her for some skanky groupie first. "And how the hell do you know about his disguise?"

"Shhh," they both said as they threw a panicked glance at the open door.

Nate stuck his head out into the corridor and glanced up and down the hallway. When he turned back around looking relieved, Jade assumed it was empty of eavesdroppers, but he still closed the door.

"I told you we're old friends. I've known from the beginning. And Nate, Jade's trustworthy, your secret won't get out."

Thank God *someone* had a high opinion of her, not like the brooding man she would have to spend her afternoons with for the next few weeks.

"I'd love to see how this meeting between you two progresses, but there are reports waiting on my desk to sign." He got up, shook Nate's hand, and whispered, "Good luck."

"I heard that!" Jade took offense.

Toby shrugged. "Actually, you both might need it." And he walked out of the room.

With Toby gone, Jade had a better look at Nate. The other night she'd been flustered and confused by what she saw, but she could have sworn his eyes were dark and dangerous. Now as she stared at him, they were a light hazel with flecks of gold.

"Your eyes are a different color. That night we met, they looked almost black." As black as his heart she'd thought. But if Toby was friends with him, he couldn't be that bad, right?

Nate nodded. "I'm not wearing contacts."

And when she'd felt his tattooed arm, his skin wasn't smooth or even hairy, it was like he'd stuck his arms into pantyhose. Now they were bare of any ink. He didn't wear a nose ring nor were there studs in his ears.

"Why go through this much trouble to change your appearance? Isn't being rich and famous something many people covet?"

"I have my reasons," he snapped.

"Well then…" She pushed her chair back and rose. Working with him was going to be a bunch of belly laughs. "I'll show you where the lessons will take place."

As she started to walk past him, he stopped her by grasping her arm. She sucked in a startled breath as heat zapped her skin and traveled through her body. He dropped her arm as if he also felt the effects.

"It's a long, boring story. You wouldn't be interested." This time he'd softened his tone.

Wouldn't be interested. Wanna make a bet? But it was his story, and if he didn't want to share with the class, that was his business.

They stood almost chest to chest, staring at each other. She swore Nate's gaze dropped to her lips, and she thought he might kiss her. Then he opened the door as if the moment had never happened.

But as she made to pass, Nate's gaze traveled to her chest. Wow, if he was trying to turn up the sexual attraction, he had another thing coming. They were in a primary school!

"You like a bit of sauce?"

She frowned. *What the hell did that mean?* "If this is some new term for sexual favors I haven't heard of before, you're out of luck. Do you even know where we are? I suppose women give you sex no matter the location. Well, not me, buddy."

For a moment Nate's eyes widened, then he pointed to her top and chuckled. "There's sauce on your shirt."

She looked down at the stain and mentally gave herself a forehead slap. How could she forget about the stab wound?

"Freckles, for a primary school teacher, you sure have a dirty mind." He snickered and walked out of the room.

Jade stood for a beat, a scathing response nowhere to be found, then she followed him out.

Nate walked through the corridor, laughing on the inside. He had a feeling if he laughed out loud, Jade would yell at him. And he would keep to himself that he was totally checking out her breasts. The soft fabric with a button popped open showed the edges of a white, sensible-looking bra. A stab of lust had hit him hard, and he'd had to resist the urge to kiss her.

He scrubbed a hand over his face. What the hell was he thinking? He had women at concerts flashing him with impressive-sized breasts all the time, and not one of them had left an impression or even made him want to look twice. So why did this tiny woman, with her big temper, turn him on so much?

"The school hall is this way," she said with a clipped tone as she brushed past him.

He watched her hips sway has she stormed into what

he assumed would be the music room. Now he couldn't take his eyes off her slim hips and imagined what it would be like to hold them in his hands while she rocked on top—

Dammit, what was going on? How long had it been since he'd last had sex?

If he needed to ask himself that question, it had been way too long. Being on tour didn't give him the opportunity, regardless of all the phone numbers slipped to him. With his disguise, it couldn't happen. Nor did he want some groupie who'd do about anyone with a guitar in their hand. And on his downtime, when he'd packed away the disguise, which wasn't often, he'd be in his hotel room playing music completely different to what his band played. He played music he loved, music that flowed through his veins and made his heart pump with excitement.

He just needed to get laid, and this blazing hot redhead was a huge temptation. But if they would be working together, it probably wasn't the best idea. Was it even allowed? But their working arrangement was only temporary; surely that wouldn't be breaking any school rules? Hell, Jade didn't even like him, so why the hell did he think she'd want to sleep with him?

"So, this is where we'll be conducting the lessons," she said, interrupting his thoughts. "We've had instruments donated. They're not in the greatest condition, but we'll just have to make do."

Nate decided he needed to get his mind out of the gutter and concentrate on why he was there. He inspected the instruments. "You're not wrong about them not being in the greatest condition." He picked up an acoustic guitar with two strings missing and a small hole in the timber. "No one can play on this."

"I'll need to get a few things repaired and tuned—"

"It's not worth spending the money. This is all garbage. Whoever *donated* these was probably going to throw them out anyway. You've saved them the tip fees." He turned to find a stricken expression on Jade's face. "Sorry," he added to soften the blow. He didn't mean to upset her.

Then the wounded expression changed, a splash of red colored her cheeks, and her mouth slammed into a thin line. "When I see Brian, I will rip his head off! He promised me these were easily fixed. I should never have trusted him. He has shifty, little beady insect eyes." She dropped onto a nearby stool, slumping her shoulders in defeat like she wasn't only seconds ago about to decapitate someone. "So, I guess we won't be needing your help. The school can't buy the instruments I need."

It bothered him seeing her so upset. Nor did he want to deprive a child of free lessons. "I'll buy them."

She sat up straight on the seat. "What?"

"I was going to give you the stuff from my grand-mother's garage, but why not just buy new stuff?" It wasn't like he couldn't afford it. "Give me a list of whatever you need."

"Are you serious?" Standing up, she raced over to him. He nodded.

"Oh my God. That's so generous. Thank you." And

she threw her arms around him.

It wasn't anything other than appreciation, but the contact blasted through his body, making him hot and extremely turned on. To keep her from pulling away too soon, he wrapped his arms around her too.

The top of her head barely reached his chin, but they seemed to fit perfectly together. And as he pulled her in a little tighter, she didn't complain. But after a beat, like she realized the embrace was taking longer than necessary, she stepped back.

Clearing her throat, she said, "Thanks again."

"I'm happy to do it."

A few strands of red curls broke away from her ponytail and framed her round face. God, she was cute and sexy and passionate. He wanted to get his hands on her, touch her, and taste her smooth, creamy skin. Wanted to watch her face flush red and her freckles pop when he touched her in all her sensitive places.

Unable to stop himself, he tucked a wayward strand behind her ear, his finger caressing the side of her face. She drew in a quick breath, and her gaze dropped to his lips before she stepped further away. It was probably a good idea she put distance between them. A primary school music hall wasn't the best place to make out.

"Get my number from Toby and text me your list."

Jade just nodded, her eyes looking a little wild, as if the attraction sparking between them surprised her.

He walked toward the door. When he reached it, he turned back. "I look forward to the kiss you promised me, Freckles." And he left as her jaw hit the floor.

Chapter 5

"*I*'ve fallen truly, madly, crazily in lust," Jade announced with a long sigh to her friends Lauren and Ava while they sat in a booth at Jovi's Pub.

It was the third margarita she consumed that helped the words spring free. It wasn't like Jade to drink more than one glass on a school night, but after the day she'd had, all because of a very sexy rock star slash music teacher, she deserved it.

Lauren and Ava both paused with their glasses at their lips, then put them down on the table. Ava was the first to speak. "I'm loving the sound of this. Please continue."

"You know how I want to provide music lessons for the students at my school?" When they both nodded, she said, "Well, Toby has found someone who will teach the classes for a few weeks."

"That's wonderful, Jade. You've wanted to do this for your kids for so long," Lauren said, smiling.

"Yeah, yeah. Music, kids… It's great, I'm happy for you, but get to the good part," Ava insisted.

"Getting lessons for them *is* the good part." When Ava rolled her eyes, Jade added, "I thought that would interest you considering you're about to give birth to one."

Ava took a quick sip of her sparkling water, then lovingly rubbed her swollen belly and smiled. "I'd still prefer talking about lust than kids. If I turn out like Lauren after I have this baby, my kid will be what I'll always be talking about. So, I want to gossip about the good stuff before that happens."

"Hey!" Lauren protested.

"It's true, but I love my godson, so it's allowed."

"Well, thanks for your permission." Sarcasm dripped from Lauren's tone as she sipped her drink.

Ava squirmed in the seat and placed a hand on her lower back. "God, this kid better come out soon. I'm the size of a whale."

Jade and Lauren rolled their eyes at the *whale* reference. Only a couple of weeks away from giving birth and she could still step onto a catwalk like a high-fashion runway model and turn heads. No swollen ankles, no puffy face, beautiful shiny hair, and a compact belly. It didn't surprise Jade that Ava looked so good; she always looked amazing.

"I should go home and give Nick a bit of *lust*, it might bring on labor."

More like love, Jade thought. Ava had always avoided relationships with a passion and she'd never believed in marriage, but now she was happily married to her old teenage boyfriend, Nick Williams. And she had never looked happier.

"But before I do that, tell us who you've fallen truly, madly, crazily in lust with."

"As I was saying, Toby found someone to teach, and…he's freaking gorgeous." She couldn't tell them he was more than a music teacher, even though she was dying to. She'd made a promise. It wasn't her secret to tell. "*And* not only is he gorgeous, he's buying new instruments because the ones we have are crap."

"Wow, Jade, that's so generous. What does he do for a living that he can afford that?" Lauren asked.

"Umm…something in the music industry." She shrugged like she wasn't sure. God, she hated lying to her friends. A sickly feeling spread through her stomach.

"Can we get back to the lust part of the conversation and what you're going to do about it?" Ava tapped an impatient hand on the table.

"There's nothing more to say. I'm not going to do anything about it. We'll be working together."

"So? Office hook-ups happen all the time," Ava said.

"It's not an office. It's a primary school," Jade corrected.

"You won't be getting it on in the classroom. What you do after hours is no one's business. And you said he was only teaching for a few weeks, he's not a permanent staff member. So, unleash your lust-crazed body on him."

Jade laughed. "I've only just met the guy."

Ava shrugged like that meant nothing.

"Does he feel the same way?" Lauren, always the more sensible one, asked.

Does he? When he touched the side of her face, she could have sworn heat shot from his hazel-brown eyes. "I think he was checking out my boobs." She frowned. "Well, I thought he was, but it was the sauce I spilled on my top."

Her friends burst out laughing. "What boobs? Must have been the sauce," Ava joked.

Jade crossed her arms over her chest like she needed to protect her assets, no matter how small. "I'm deeply offended you said that," she said stiffly.

"I'm sorry." Ava wiped the tears at the edges of her eyes. "We know how sensitive you are." But Ava didn't look sorry.

"Ava, stop teasing her," Lauren said, not able to hide her own grin. "It's not every day Jade falls in lust. Maybe this music teacher will be the love of her life."

Jade made a small choking sound and shook her head. Her hair was down, and the curls bounced around her shoulders. "*Love of my life?* Nah-uh. No way. You know I can't let that happen."

Ava blew out a long breath. "Yes, the family *curse.* We hear about it every time you're with someone new. You end it before it gets serious, because you think they'll leave—"

"I *know* they'll leave."

"Jade—"

"You both think it's crazy, but this curse placed on my family over a hundred years ago is true. The women will never be happy in love, because when they fall for some-one, the men leave. I have proof." It sounded crazy to Jade too. Normally she wouldn't believe in hocus-pocus stuff, but her family's doomed relationships were real.

"What? A couple of failed marriages and broken engagements—nothing I don't see in my law firm every day. But you know this already. I can't keep repeating myself." Ava threw a look at Lauren. "What have you got to add?"

"If Ava can fall in love and be happily married, then you can too," Lauren offered.

Instead of taking offense, Ava lifted her glass in a toast. "So very true."

"I know I can fall in love." She'd come close a couple of times but ended it before she got her heart broken. "It's them sticking around that's the problem."

Ava threw up her hands in surrender. "I give up. Nothing we say will ever convince you. But wouldn't you like to see if a guy will believe you're worth sticking around for?"

She would love that more than anything. But if her own father didn't love her mother and their family enough to stay when they'd all been so happy, how did she expect anyone else to? The curse was too strong.

But before Jade answered, the sound of a guitar being strummed caught her attention. Turning in the seat to look at the small stage anyone rarely performed on, she saw the man she'd fallen truly, madly, crazily in lust with.

Nate sat on a timber stool, his feet propped up on the footrests with a shiny, black guitar perched on his thigh.

His nimble fingers worked their way over the strings like he was warming them up. Then, as if he felt her gaze, he lifted his head and searched through the small Tuesday night crowd until he spotted her. Giving her a wink and a crooked smile, he began playing a tune.

Jade's chest squeezed tight. God, why did she always have such a reaction to a mere smile from him? She had to remind herself he could also be a big jerk. He'd threatened, no *promised* her a lawsuit if she spilled his secret.

And then he sang. Words so deep, slow, and melodious came pouring out of him, stealing the attention of the crowd. They paused in their drinking and chatter to watch and listen, entranced by his performance. And Jade couldn't pull her gaze away either.

He sang about love, loss, and dreams in such a raw and heartfelt way. The emotions in the lyrics poured through her like he was telling her story.

When he finished his set, the crowd got to their feet and applauded. He waved his thanks and made his way to the bar.

"Wow," Lauren said as they sat back down. "He's amazing."

"He sure was, and hot too," Ava said. "I wonder who he is."

"He's my new music teacher," Jade explained, not taking her eyes off Nate as he pulled back on a beer.

Ava chuckled. "Oh boy…you're in *big trouble*."

Jade turned to look at Ava. "Why do you say that?" But deep down she already believed the same thing.

"You'll be working with that sexy man? How are you

going to do so without wanting to put your hands all over him?" Ava asked.

God, she *was* in big trouble. But all she had to do was remember he could be a jerk, right? A big one who's buying her kids new musical equipment and sings like a freaking angel. Yeah, she was in big trouble.

"A class filled with children should help to control your urges," Lauren supplied.

Thank goodness Lauren always made her see clearly. Of course, she couldn't get kinky in a music class. But after class… No. She needed to be strong. Why exactly? It wasn't professional, that was why. The school would most likely frown upon it. Her internal debate was giving her a headache.

She knocked back the remains of her drink and pushed herself from the chair. "I'm going to go talk to him."

"That's my girl," Ava cheered. "I hope you're wearing cute underwear."

Jade rolled her eyes. "I'm going to *talk* to him. That's all."

"Sounds boring." Ava huffed.

Shaking her head, Jade left her friends and weaved through the tables to get to Nate.

Nate had never felt more alive and in tune with music as he did playing in front of this crowd of roughly fifty people with only his guitar and a microphone, performing the music he loved. No amount of screaming fans or sold-out stadiums could fill him with the same joy.

Sure, he had fun playing the stuff he wrote for the band. Even got a kick out of the crowds they pulled in, but keeping the music alive was for his father's memory. But the mellow, more chilled, laid-back tunes were what got his blood pounding, the adrenalin flowing through his veins. And while he took a break from the band for a few weeks, playing at Jovi's Pub was something he intended to keep doing.

Jade slid onto a barstool next to him and said, "You're great, you'll do."

Turning toward her, he raised an eyebrow. "Excuse me?"

Tonight she wore her hair down, and it tumbled in a mass of curls past shoulders exposed in a pale yellow, strapless top. When she sat, she'd crossed her legs, and the split of her white skirt fell open, showing slender legs. His hands itched to trail along her smooth skin.

"I said...you're great, you'll do." She frowned like it hurt to repeat it.

"For what? Because I can take that to mean many different things I'm great at. Should I show you?" He grinned slowly.

For a moment Jade's gaze landed on his mouth. Oh yeah, she knew exactly where he was going with this.

"I meant..." Her voice cracked, and she cleared her throat. "I meant you'll do as a music teacher. I was teasing you."

"And I was teasing you." He smiled.

"Oh." When pink flushed her cheeks, she looked adorable. No, it was more than that. She was sexy as hell. "You're so talented. You sounded amazing."

"Thank you." He pulled back on his beer and flicked his gaze at the sport on the TV for a second in an effort to drag his thoughts away from wanting to mentally strip naked a primary school teacher.

"It's so different from what I heard the other night." She screwed up her nose.

"You didn't like the concert?"

She fidgeted with a lock of her hair. "Well...if you like that sort of music, it was great."

"But *you* don't like it." He made himself sound disappointed and loved watching her squirm. She didn't like Harvey's Territory, and he didn't care.

"Oh no, I did... It's just...different from what I'm used to," she fumbled.

Nate chuckled. "It's okay, you don't have to like it, I won't take offense."

Her shoulders slumped with relief. "It's so loud and rough. I much prefer the music you played tonight."

"Yeah, me too," he admitted.

She frowned. "So why don't you play more of it on stage?"

"It doesn't exactly fit in with the band's brand."

Someone called Jade's name. The friends she'd been sitting with signaled they were leaving. She mouthed *give me a minute*. But they gestured for her to stay, and the pregnant one gave her a salacious wink before they walked out.

Jade groaned and shook her head. "Sorry about that. She's not exactly subtle." And like she wanted to change the subject, she quickly said, "They loved your music too. And don't worry, I promise I didn't say anything," she whispered.

He leaned closer, and he could see her pulse pounding in her neck. Thoughts of trailing his tongue along it filled his mind, but he pushed them aside. "About me being Hannah Montana?"

Biting her bottom lip, she giggled. "I *should* feel bad about that." The laughter on her face showed no sign of being sorry.

"I can't believe you compared me to some Disney character." But she hadn't been completely wrong. He was like the male version of the singer, only with better songs.

"Well, you weren't exactly nice to me."

"I thought you were a—"

"Groupie. Yes, I know. But I'm not."

And he liked that about her. "So, if you weren't backstage chasing musicians, why were you stalking the corridors?"

"Like I told you that night, I was looking for my cousin and I got lost."

"I hear a lot of stories about getting *lost*. I'm sorry I didn't believe you. I assume you found your cousin?"

"Yes, thank goodness. Just in time too. She was making plans to fly to Vegas and elope with your drummer."

That startled a laugh from him. "Elope? As in getting married?"

"Yes. And if I hadn't stopped them, she would have made the biggest mistake of her life. He would only have left her."

"Although I doubt any marriage would work under those circumstances, Mike gets crazy ideas sometimes and has eloped twice already. He wasn't thinking with the *brain* in his head but with the one in his pants. It was bound to fall apart," he said.

"Even if they were deeply in love, this one wouldn't work because she's—" Her lips slammed shut.

"She's what?" he urged.

"It's getting late. I should go." She slid off the barstool, looking like she was about to bolt.

He held on to her wrist, stopping her from leaving. "Why wouldn't it have worked? What's wrong with your cousin?" Already married? Really a man? A dozen crazy reasons ran through his head. Who did Mike almost marry?

She blew a strand of hair from her eyes, and when it only fell back on her face, she pulled her wrist from his grip, reached into her pocket, and pulled out a hair tie. Twisting it into some kind of bun, she secured it on top of her head, exposing the smooth skin of her neck.

"If I tell you, you'll think I'm crazy."

"Why would I think you're crazy? Trust me, I've heard a lot of wild shit. What you tell me can't be that bad. Does your cousin have webbed feet or something?"

She rolled her eyes. "No. It's nothing like that."

Sliding back on the barstool, she arranged her skirt over her legs. Damn, he wished she hadn't covered them.

"If I tell you, promise me you won't laugh," she said.

Making the sign of a cross over his chest, he nodded. "Promise."

She took a deep breath and said, "She's cursed. Well, my whole family is."

What the... "Your family is cursed?"

"Yes."

"What does that mean, and how does this affect your cousin eloping?" This was weirder than if she'd told him she had webbed feet.

She narrowed her eyes and searched his face like she was deciding if she could tell him or not. Then she drew in a deep breath. "Over a hundred years ago, a witch in Ireland put a curse on my family. And since then, the men who get involved with Brennan women—that's my family name—leave. It's usually before they get married, but it can happen after too."

He forced his features to stay straight-faced, because he knew if he so much as cracked a smile she'd walk. He'd been wrong about hearing crazy stuff—*this* would have to be the craziest thing he'd ever heard.

"A witch?"

"Yes." Her face remained expressionless.

Christ, she was serious. "And this curse happens often?"

"Well, it hasn't for a while until Liz got dumped at the altar. Going with her to your concert was a way of getting her out of the house and having fun again. By the way, she loves your band. I'd never heard of you until that night." Her eyes grew round, and she covered her mouth. "Sorry."

This time he laughed. "Don't be. It explains the lack of enthusiasm."

Jade laughed too, and he loved the sound.

"You don't really believe in this curse, do you?" Nate asked.

He must have looked skeptical, because Jade's laughter died. "I knew you wouldn't believe me, no one does."

"Not that I don't believe you…" He sure as hell didn't, but he was keeping his mouth shut about his opinion. "It's just not something you hear every day. Is there any way you can break it?"

With a stiff expression, she blew out a long breath. "If there was, we would have broken it by now."

"I guess that was a dumb question. Sorry."

Her features softened. "No, I'm sorry. I should know by now to keep this to myself."

God, how many people did she tell this story to? "I'll be honest, witches and curses are up there with Santa and the Easter Bunny. I don't believe in them, but you do, so I'm not going to judge."

"You don't believe in Santa?" She gave him a playful grin.

"Many people believe in unusual things." He had a mate who swore he'd seen Bigfoot. But he'd been drunk at the time. "You don't think this will happen to you, do you?" he asked.

"It will, I'm a Brennan." She looked at him as if he were an idiot after she'd explained it to him.

"What have you tried to break it?"

She gave him a blank look. "Tried?"

"Yeah, like...burning incense or dancing naked under a full moon." That he'd love to see. Her alabaster skin glowing in the moonlight and her red hair falling in waves down her back. "Or it could be like those fairy tales where Prince Charming kisses the princess and breaks the evil witch's curse."

"And who's the lucky prince who will kiss me so we can live happily ever after? *You?*"

Backing up, he nearly fell off his chair. She slid off the stool. This time he didn't stop her. Something in her boiling expression told him he might get slapped if he tried.

"No, I didn't think so. I'll let you know when we're ready to start the lessons." With that, she stormed out of the pub.

Dammit, he'd pissed her off again. And boy did she look sexy as hell.

Chapter 6

*T*he next morning, while the children played during recess, Jade was setting up the classroom for art. She banged tubes of paint on the desks as she rehashed Nate's reaction about her beliefs on the family curse.

It shouldn't surprise her that another person thought she'd lost her mind. She'd been laughed at and teased by family and friends but never let it bother her like this. So why did it feel like a kick in the gut when he looked at her with amusement in his eyes?

Another paint tube slammed the desk. Maybe she was just over being ridiculed, and he was the last straw.

"What has the poor paint done to you to deserve such abuse?"

Whipping around, Jade found Toby standing in the doorway.

"I'm pretending it's someone's head," she said, this

time placing down the rest of the tubes with a little less anger.

Toby laughed. "I hope it's not one of your students."

"My students are angels."

Toby lifted an eyebrow.

"Most of the time. It's your *friend* who I'd love to throw this at."

She was pleased that after last night, she'd fallen *out* of truly, madly, crazily in lust. Yep, no heart flutters or funny, tingly feelings. Well, the tingly part when she thought of him—which happened a lot—was still around, but it was probably something she might need to see a gynecologist for.

"That *friend* of mine has just sent you a delivery."

"Already? I only sent him a text with a list two days ago."

"I guess he has connections. There's a truck outside waiting to be unloaded." Toby pointed over his shoulder.

Racing to the window, she peered out. "Oh, wow. That's a big truck."

"The driver wants to know where you want it all to go."

She glanced at the clock on the wall. "Recess is almost over. Can you watch my kids for a few minutes?" When Toby nodded, she added, "Don't forget to tell them to put their paint shirts on." With that, she ran out the door.

When she reached the truck, she skidded to a stop and tried to keep her excitement under control. She couldn't believe the kids were not only getting free music lessons, they'd get to play on brand-new instruments.

A man with a clipboard approached, and two other men went to the back of the truck and opened the doors. "You Jade Brennan?" Clipboard Man asked. Without waiting for her to answer, he passed her the delivery docket she needed to sign.

Quickly scribbling her name, she then glanced at the equipment being unloaded, not able to hide her smile.

"Where would you like us to put them?" one man asked.

"Follow me." Once in the hall she pointed to a corner of the room. "Put them there."

The man holding a couple of guitars put them where he was instructed and scratched his head. "You'll need a lot more room than that spot. The truck is piled with the stuff."

And he wasn't wrong.

After they unloaded everything and left, Jade stood dumbstruck in the hall. Yamaha keyboards, Gibson and Fender acoustic and electric guitars, Pearl drum kits, every kind of wind and string instrument, tambourines, xylophones, and microphones. There were also music books and stands and things she didn't even recognize. There was more than one of each instrument and in different sizes. She assumed to accommodate for the smaller and bigger kids.

This was musical heaven, and Nate did this for them. Now she was back to being truly, madly, crazily in lust. Who was she kidding? It had never left.

He'd gone beyond anything she could ever have imagined. She needed to thank him for such generosity. But she decided to write it in a text, because if she called him, she'd probably say something silly like declaring her love for him, and she'd already offered up her first-born child, so that wouldn't be good.

Pulling her phone out of her pocket, she typed a message.

Thanks for the new music school. I hear Juilliard is locating here soon.

It didn't take long for a reply. *I'd much prefer the School of Rock.*

Jade laughed. *Thank you. It's amazing. The kids will love it.*

You're welcome. Would you like to have dinner with me tonight?

Jade's heart fluttered behind her ribs. Then another text came through.

We can discuss a program.

Of course it was to discuss music. How dumb was she to think, even for a second, it was for anything else? She texted back a time and a place.

I'm looking forward to it, he replied.

The flutter was back, so she quickly sent him a thumbs-up emoji, because even through a text, she might send something stupid like hearts and kisses.

Nate chuckled as he put his mobile phone in his pocket.

"I haven't seen such a happy smile on your face in a long time. I'd love to thank the woman who put it there," his seventy-nine-year-old grandmother said as she put two cups of coffee on the kitchen table and sat next to him.

Dressed in bright red tights and a tight, black tank top, her silver hair with pale pink streaks was pulled up in a messy ponytail. She looked nothing like a typical grandmother should. Well, what he thought a typical grandmother should look like.

"I smile all the time, and why would you think it's because of a woman?"

"You've hardly cracked a decent one since you've come home. I would've thought you'd be happy to see me at least." She huffed. "And a man only looks like that over a woman," she said and blew into her steaming cup of coffee.

"I am happy to see you. I've missed you."

"So why the long face when you visit? Are you missing the tour and your band mates already?"

"As much as I love the band, living with them almost twenty-four hours a day for three months straight isn't always fun."

He needed space. It was good to have a break from them. They'd tried convincing him to go to the states with them, but being back in his hometown for a few weeks was where he needed to be. New York didn't hold the greatest of memories.

"Fi-Fi." His grandmother had refused to be called anything grandmotherly, and they'd come up with the nickname when he moved in with her. "Are *you* not happy I'm home?"

He'd never thought to ask if she wanted him around.

He'd rented his own house, but did he come over too often? She was a woman who enjoyed a busy lifestyle; maybe he was getting in the way.

She waved her hand in the air. "Of course I love having you home. But you seem lost, like you don't know what to do with yourself, and a little sad if I'm going to be honest with you."

When was she ever *not* honest with him? When he needed to stay grounded, she held him down with concrete boots.

"I guess I'm not used to having so much downtime." And the thought of playing music he didn't feel pulsing through his veins made it harder and harder to be enthusiastic about getting back on tour. "While I'm in town, I'm helping Toby out with after-school music lessons."

"That's wonderful. He always had great ideas for that school."

"Not Toby's idea. One of his teachers came up with the idea."

His grandmother searched his face in a way that always made him feel like she could read his thoughts. And most times she'd get it right. "This teacher's the one who's put the smile on your face."

It wasn't a question. Damn, how did she do that? After all these years he still hadn't figured it out. Maybe Jade was right and there really were witches.

"You'll have to bring her over sometime. Anyone who can make my boy beam from ear to ear is worth getting to know."

"She sent me a funny text. That's all," Nate said.

"Will you be working with this teacher?"

"Yes."

Fi-Fi smirked. "This will be interesting," she said as she rose from her chair. "Well, I'm off to my pole dancing class. I'll see you later."

Yeah, she definitely wasn't like any grandmother he knew.

Chapter 7

*J*ade tried on about ten different outfits before deciding on a pale blue dress with spaghetti straps that flowed just below the knees. Tempted to call Lauren or Ava for ideas, she quickly decided against it. It was only a business meeting, and they'd make it out to be something more. Especially after she'd confessed about being in lust with the guy.

She'd already received a text message from Ava asking if she'd taken things further with him that night at Jovi's. No, nothing happened, because he'd thought she was a crazy person and she'd walked out on him. And nothing would happen, because...well, it just couldn't. Could it? She shook her head with confusion.

She gave one last look at her reflection in the mirror, reminding herself they were *only* meeting for dinner to discuss a music program. Nothing more. Then she grabbed her keys and left the house.

When she arrived at the restaurant Lorenzo's Table,

she spotted Nate straight away. It was like her senses were drawn to him no matter how crowded the room. When he saw her, he waved and smiled, and her knees shook. Trying to walk balancing on heels was always a challenge, trying to do it on unsteady legs was dangerous. Thankfully, she made it to the table with no mishaps.

"You look great," he said as he rose and pulled out her chair.

He didn't look so bad himself. A white dress shirt rolled up to the elbows exposed tanned, ropey arms. A few opened buttons showed the tan continued onto his chest. His hair looked damp from a recent shower and finger-combed. God, he was gorgeous.

"I wasn't sure if you would show up," he said.

Jade flicked her wrist to glance at her watch. "Am I late?"

He shook his head. "I've pissed you off a time or two."

"You didn't piss me off."

He arched an eyebrow.

"Okay, maybe you did a *little*," she admitted.

He chuckled, and her heart hammered.

"But after your donation to the school, I couldn't stay mad. So, thank you."

"It was my pleasure." Hearing the word *pleasure* roll off his lips conjured images that had nothing to do with violins and drums.

A waitress showed up at their table, forcing Jade to think of food instead of fun things with Nate. She gave the woman her order of pasta carbonara and a glass of shiraz.

When the waitress turned to take Nate's order she paused with her pencil on her notepad. Instead of asking for his order, she narrowed her eyes and stared at him for a beat. "You look familiar. Where do I know you from?"

Nate shrugged his shoulders. "I've just come into town."

She tapped her pencil on the pad. "Are you an actor? I'm sure I've seen you on TV."

Oh God. Was this waitress going to expose Nate's secret? And how could he sit there so calmly while she was giving him a thorough inspection?

"I've been on a health food commercial," he said, smiling. "That must be where you've seen me."

"Hmm, must be." But she didn't look convinced. And before she asked any more questions, Nate gave her his order and she left.

Feeling a little unsettled that Nate's secret could've been exposed, Jade placed her elbows on the table and leaned forward. "Does that happen often?"

"No. Hardly ever. I can always put them off track if it does."

"Have you done a health food commercial?"

"Nope."

They both laughed.

"I thought she would work it out," Jade said more seriously.

"My disguise is solid. Unless my wig gets caught in someone's fingers." He grinned.

"It must be exhausting keeping up with the double identity."

His expression closed.

"Sorry. It's none of my business. I'm not that interested anyway." She began rearranging the cutlery.

When she looked up, his dark, moody face watched her closely.

Curiosity getting the better of her, she sighed and said, "I *am* interested. Why the disguise?"

The corner of his lips twitched into a smile. "Will you ever leave it alone?"

"Probably not. I can't discover something so huge and not know anything about why."

"I don't want to be famous," he said flatly.

"Isn't that the dream of every guy who joins a band?"

Their meals arrived before Nate could reply. Placing their plates on the table, the waitress searched his face, still trying to pinpoint where she'd seen him, probably not satisfied with his health food commercial answer.

"Can I get your autograph?" the woman asked. "Just in case you become famous."

Jade bit her trembling lips to stop from laughing as she watched Nate sign a napkin.

When she left, Jade couldn't hold it in any longer. God, if she only knew who she just served dinner to. "This will bug her all night."

He laughed too. "She'll forget all about me soon enough."

He quickly dug into his plate of veal scallopini, and Jade had to wait before she could ask more questions. Impatient fingers tapped the table.

"Why don't you want to be famous?" she finally asked.

He looked up, dabbed his mouth with a napkin, and took a long swallow of wine. "I'm not comfortable with the attention."

"On stage you appear extremely comfortable with it. In fact, you looked like you were born to be there."

"In a way I kind of was."

She frowned. "What do you mean?"

"You have no idea about the history of my music and my family, do you?"

She shook her head. "Sorry, like I told you, I'd never heard of your band until the night I went to the concert."

"Have you heard of Cold Revenge?" he asked.

"Yes, my dad was a fan."

"My dad was Liam Harvey, the lead singer."

She took a moment to put the fuzzy puzzle pieces together. She remembered years ago her dad mentioning the lead singer had passed away. How, she couldn't remember.

"My parents died when I was twelve...overdose," he added before she could ask.

Then he cut into his veal and took a bite. Jade gave him time to get his thoughts together.

"Their life was one big party. Every night when they were home from touring or movie sets—which wasn't often—they'd throw parties with all the major celebrities. My parents' lives really were about sex, drugs, and rock-and-roll. And fame...they loved the attention. Always wanted to be seen. They'd tip off the paparazzi when they went out in public and leaked stories about their lives." He cleared his throat. "One night at a party, they took too many drugs and mixed them with too much alcohol and never woke up."

"Oh, Nate…You must have been devastated." How horrifying for a young boy to lose both parents that way.

"I was staying at a friend's place when I saw it on TV the next day. I thought someone made it up. Dad was releasing an album, and Mum was promoting her new movie. What better way to gain publicity? Then they'd show up telling the world someone had made up a cruel joke."

Jade's heart sank for what it must have been like. "When did you find out the truth?"

"Later that day, my nanny picked me up and told me. Then two weeks later I left New York and moved to Australia to live with my grandmother Fi-Fi in Brimland Point."

Tears misted in Jade's eyes. "You must miss them."

He gave a half-hearted shrug. "When nostalgia hits, I watch an old movie of my mother's or pull out a record and listen to my father. They were too busy with their careers to spend time with their kid. It's hard to miss what you never had."

But Jade could see by his solemn expression it had affected him more than he wanted to admit.

"The only time I ever spent with my father was when he'd give me guitar lessons. He'd tell me music was in my blood. Rock-and-roll was what I needed to live and breathe."

"You must have loved those times with him."

He refilled their glasses with wine and took a deep swallow. "Not really. I could never play as well as he wanted me to. No matter how much I practiced."

Jade's heart ached for the little boy who would have tried so hard to play guitar like his father to get his praise and attention. "What about your mother? Were you close with her?"

When he smiled, no happiness reached his eyes. "From the moment I was born, she handed me over to nannies, unless she invited journalists into our home for a magazine shoot, then she was a doting mother. But I was never allowed to be photographed. Apparently, she wanted to protect my privacy. At least she did one good thing for me. It made moving to another country easier when no one recognized you were the son of two dead music and film legends."

Jade's jaw clenched. How could anyone neglect their son that way? "It must have been tough growing up like that."

"It was a long time ago." He shrugged, as if that made things okay now.

It was so not okay, but she let it drop. "So the disguise is so you can have a normal life?"

Pushing his empty plate away, he leaned his elbows on the table. "I watched my parents chase fame, and it killed them. I don't want any part of it. I love to play and sing, but I don't want to live that kind of life."

"They chose to live like that. You don't have to."

He rubbed his hand along his chin, and it made a

scratchy sound from the slight stubble. "It's a life too easy to fall into. I didn't want to take the risk. This way I can play and be Nathan Harvey, son of Liam Harvey, and then strip it all away to be plain old Nate Miller… primary school music teacher." The corner of his mouth lifted.

Taking in his good looks, there was definitely nothing *plain* about him.

"I can understand the disguise so you're out of the spotlight, but when it's off and you're living a normal life, how does that affect relationships or friendships?"

"There's too much time spent on the road to make friends. The band, my manager, and Toby are my mates. And I know they'll keep my secret. I can't risk telling anyone else."

What a lonely life it sounded like. Jade couldn't imagine being so isolated from people. "What about girl-friends? Surely you've had to tell them?"

Nate shook his head. "No girlfriends."

"None? Ever?" Her mouth dropped open.

"I'm not living like a monk. I've had women in my life. But only casually. They knew I was a musician, but that's all I could tell them. Then I'd leave to go on tour and that would be the end."

"You didn't care enough about any of those women to have more of a long-term relationship?" Jade asked.

"It never would've worked. Everything would've been based on a lie."

"If you'd fallen in love, surely you could've trusted

her?" Why did her stomach flutter with nerves waiting for the answer?

"I never stuck around long enough for feelings to get too deep."

So to live a normal life, Nate had to give up a lot. Jade wondered if it was worth the sacrifice. To lighten the mood, she said, "You must have gotten up to a lot of mischief being the son of famous parents. Aren't the kids of celebrity royalty supposed to be spoiled brats?"

Nate laughed. "When I lived in New York my nanny watched me like a hawk and rarely let me out of her sight. And when I moved in with Fi-Fi, she gave me her surname so I wouldn't be recognized. I spent all my time learning every musical instrument I could get my hands on and started a band. I never had time for anything else."

That surprised Jade. All teenagers got up to a little mischief. "You must have done some stupid stuff."

He shook his head. "Nope."

"What about parties?"

Another shake of the head.

"Sneaking alcohol out of the house and drinking so much you threw up in someone's garden?"

He raised an eyebrow.

"I've heard it happens. Not that I've done that." Jade averted her gaze for a beat. Then said, "Skinny-dipping?"

A spark of interest shot from his hazel eyes. But he shook his head. What the hell? Did he live in a monastery? Surely there was something he got up to.

She tapped her fingers on her chin. "You're not bad to

look at. Before the disguise you must have had a ton of girls chasing you."

"I had braces for three years and wore thick-lensed glasses before I had Lasik surgery."

A laugh burst from Jade. "Seriously?"

"*Seriously*," he replied with a grin.

"Wow… I'm in shock. You are full of surprises. You know, it's never too late to live a little. You should try something."

"I should?"

"Yes, but getting drunk and throwing up in a stranger's garden isn't exactly fun."

He gave her a questioning stare.

She threw up her hands and sighed. "Yes, I've done it, wasn't my proudest moment."

He chuckled.

She drummed her fingers on the table. "There's got to be something you can try that doesn't involve parties and getting drunk… Let's go skinny-dipping." The words flew out of her mouth before she had the chance to stop them.

He sat back in his chair. His eyes bore into hers, and a slow, crooked smile spread across his face. And her heart rate took off like a galloping horse. Uh-oh. She dropped herself in this one—big time.

"You want to go skinny-dipping?" His voice was low and deep, sending a warm flush over her skin.

No.

Yes.

No.

Oh God… Why did I have to blurt that out? Because she was truly, madly, crazily in lust, that's why.

"Sure, that's if you're not too chicken?" Brave words coming from someone who was shaking in her heels. He really wouldn't take her up on it, would he?

"Definitely not chicken. I'd love to see what I've missed out on." His hot gaze flicked over her. *Oh boy!*

"Okay then, we'll have to fit it in some time while you're in town."

Maybe he'd forget about her stupid suggestion. But *why* was it stupid again? She'd get to see what was under his clothes, and she didn't think she'd be disappointed with what she'd find. It was a brilliant idea.

"Tonight," Nate said.

"Excuse me?" Jade choked.

"We're both free now. The weather's warm. Why wait?" His voice rumbled and all her girly parts tingled with lusty excitement.

Why wait? Because she didn't mean to blurt it out. But now it was out there… Was she wearing her good underwear? Yes, she'd chosen a lacy blue set like she knew they would be on display. As of two days ago, she was freshly waxed, so all good there too.

She drew in a deep, shuddery breath. "Let's do it."

He signaled to the waitress. "The bill please."

Chapter 8

*I*f Jade was surprised by Nate's uneventful teenage years, *he* was shocked by how much she'd gotten him to reveal about his childhood. His grandmother and Toby were the only ones who knew what growing up with his parents was like. Not even his band members knew the full story.

He hadn't talked about his past in years. It only brought up harsh memories. But earlier when he did, there wasn't the stabbing pain in his chest that happened whenever he talked about his parents. What was it about Jade that made him feel comfortable enough to open up?

He'd have to wonder about that another time. Because he had better things to think about now, like Jade's skinny-dipping bomb. He'd be an idiot to refuse.

Moving at groundbreaking speed, he'd paid the bill and had them standing outside on the footpath. He hoped she wouldn't change her mind, and it killed him to ask, "Are you sure you want to do this?"

She nibbled on her plump bottom lip, a lip he desperately wanted to taste, and anticipation drummed through his body.

She straightened her shoulders. "Someone has to help you live out your teenage years. Come on," she said, linking her fingers through his. "I know just the place."

After crossing the road, they strolled along a strip of Brimland Point where small boutiques and cafés lined the street. The smell of the ocean nearby wafted through the sultry night air as they continued to walk in silence.

Nate hadn't let go of Jade's hand; it was smaller than his callused one, and heat surged through her from the innocent touch. But what wasn't so innocent was the fact she was going skinny-dipping with a man she barely knew. And it didn't make her want to run and hide. It only turned up the heat to the next level.

When they reached the beach, the fresh ocean breeze did nothing to relieve her feverish skin. She removed her heels and curled her toes in the cool sand and waited for Nate to take off his shoes.

"We need to walk past those beach houses and rock pools. There's a section that's partially secluded." Her voice shook. Why was she so nervous? She'd done this a bunch of times as a teenager. Well, maybe not a bunch, but once or twice. And never with boys. *Oh shit.*

They trudged along the soft sand, and all too soon, they reached the section of the beach surrounded by boulders. Jade's stomach churned, and she flicked a nervous glance over her shoulder at the houses in the distance. Hopefully, they were far enough away not to be seen. Thankfully, the pale light thrown from the full moon kept them in relative darkness.

Nate sat on the sand and Jade followed. Taking a deep breath of the briny air, she tried to calm her jittery nerves.

The ocean was more like a lake and only a ripple of tiny waves hit the shore.

"Do you think there are any sharks?" Nate asked.

Jade gave a startled laugh. "Oh God, I hope not."

"I've watched *Jaws*, I know what happens when the beautiful woman convinces the sexy guy to go skinny-dipping—"

"You're calling *yourself* sexy?" She made a scoffing sound.

Oh yes, he was the sexiest man she'd ever seen, but she'd keep that to herself. She didn't want him to get an inflated ego. *And* he'd called her beautiful. Her heart pounded.

"Don't worry, little girl, I'm here to protect you," Jade teased.

He laughed and stood up. The moon cast enough light for Jade to see him unbuttoning his shirt. Once off, it floated to the ground. He had wide shoulders, narrow hips, and hard abs. Tattooed over his left pec was an intricate design of musical notes, roses, and a guitar. It was beautiful—he was beautiful. Her breath quickened.

Next, Nate unbuttoned the fly of his jeans, pushed them down slowly, and stepped out of them, tossing them on top of his rumpled shirt. Was she going swimming or watching the strip show *Thunder from Down Under*? Where was her wallet so she could put a twenty in his underwear? That thought made her focus on the tight, thin, black fabric hugging him and the impressive bulge straining behind it. He deserved more than a twenty.

Jade wanted to burn this erotic display in her memory because she doubted she'd ever witness anything so spectacular again.

His chuckle rumbled into the night air, and she lifted her gaze and stared into his hooded eyes. "Like what you see?"

"You're all right. You might need a few more workouts at the gym though."

He threw his head back and laughed. Obviously not taking offense at her criticism, he stood unselfconsciously with hands on hips, gazing at her with a sexy gleam in his eyes. "It's your turn."

"My turn?" *Yes, stupid. Who else is on the beach?*

"Someone's wearing too many clothes to go skinny-dipping… If it's me, should I take more off?" He raised a questioning eyebrow as he slid his fingers in the elastic waistband of his undies.

"No!" she yelled.

Yes! she wanted to scream.

He flashed her one of his heart-stopping smiles.

Oh Lord.

Rising, she dusted the sand off her butt. She could do this. Men had seen her naked before. Not many, but enough to know she wasn't a prude. All she needed to do was take off one thing at a time. Nothing to it.

She reached around her back to unzip her dress. But as she gave the zipper a tug, it got stuck on the fabric and wouldn't slide down. She pulled a little harder, but it only made it stick more.

"Umm, my zipper is caught. I need help." She turned her back to him.

As he stepped closer, even though they weren't touching, heat from his body surrounded her. Slowly, he pushed her hair from her shoulder and his fingers brushed the side of her neck. Her body quivered and goose bumps exploded over her skin. Such a simple act had her turned on in a not so simple way.

After a beat, the dress gaped open. A cool breeze rippled across her overheated skin.

"It's fixed." Nate's voice sounded husky and unsteady.

Was he as affected as she was?

Holding her dress to her chest, she turned and met his hot gaze and found her answer. "Do we...should we... everything off or..." The words clogged in her tight throat.

"How about we leave our underwear on? It's my first time, I'm a little shy." He smirked.

She breathed a sigh of relief and knew damn well he wasn't *shy*. "You go ahead. I'll meet you there in a second." She needed a moment to calm her jittery nerves.

"Great, so I'm shark bait." He laughed. "Don't be long."

His gaze traveled over her body, and even though

she still held onto her dress, he looked at her as if she was completely naked. Then he jogged to the water's edge.

Under the soft light she could see the muscle definition in his back as it dipped above the roundness of his butt as he hurdled over the small, breaking waves. Then he stood in waist deep water for a moment, looking like he was offering himself up like a sacrifice to the moon goddess, before diving in. The reflection of the moon rippled over the water's surface. A moment later, he reappeared and shook his head. Tiny drops of water sprayed off his hair like little flecks of diamonds. She'd never witnessed anything so goddamn sexy.

He waved to her. "The water's perfect."

Okay, she couldn't stand there all night. She did a quick scan of the area, and once satisfied no one was around, she took a deep breath and dropped the dress. Should she walk or run? Fully aware of Nate's gaze on her, she settled for a quick walk. There was a high risk if she ran, she'd fall flat on her face.

Nate watched as Jade shimmied out of her dress. Smooth, creamy breasts sat high in a lacy, pale blue bra. Her petite body was perfectly shaped in all the right places. Christ, how was he supposed to control himself?

As the water reached her belly, she sucked in a startled breath, and her nipples bore through its lacy confinement. He had to stop himself from groaning out loud. Thank

God the water was around his waist so she couldn't see how she was affecting him.

When she waded closer, he asked, "What do we do now?" God, he hoped it was what was on his mind.

Sliding her hands onto his chest, she smiled. "We swim." Then she pushed him away, laughing as he fell under the water.

When he resurfaced, he wiped the water from his face. Jade was floating on her back, lightly kicking her legs and swaying her arms with the water swirling around her body.

"I might never have skinny-dipped before, but I reckon it should be a lot more fun than just swimming. If I'm to live out a teenage experience, I'd want it to include doing something with the naked woman I'm with."

Jade stopped floating and splashed him playfully. "I'm not naked."

"That's too bad." He grinned.

She feigned a shocked expression then said, "We can have a swimming race?"

He shook his head. "Boring."

"See who can hold their breath under the water the longest?" she suggested with a playful smile.

"I might be new to skinny-dipping, but I have a gut feeling water games aren't usually involved." He paddled closer. "I have an idea."

"You do?" Her eyes widened.

Her smile dropped, and her tongue darted out to lick the water from her lips. God, if only she knew how much he wanted her right now.

Pulling himself together, he said, "For starters, I'd want to put my hands on you."

"Sounds interesting," she said with a throaty voice.

He slid his palms onto her hips, pulling her closer, and water swirled around them. A tremble racked through her body. Her skin, slippery and cool under his touch, melded against him.

"Then, I'd want to lick the salt from your skin," he said.

"Too much salt is bad for your health," she said on a shuddery breath.

"Freckles, I'll take my chances." He bent his head and nibbled at her shoulder then traced the sweet curve of her neck, licking off the salt with his tongue. "Is this how you used to skinny-dip?" he mumbled against her racing pulse.

"It's not the way I remember it." She sighed and tilted her head to the side.

"Next, I'd want a kiss." He lifted his head and took in the sight of her. Red, curly hair dripped wet around her creamy shoulders. He'd never seen anything so beautiful.

"A kiss?"

"I recall you owe me one. And your first born too, but I'll let you keep your baby."

"Well, I always pay my debts." Her gaze dropped to his mouth.

He needed to taste her and couldn't hold back a moment longer. He lowered his head and kissed her. Soft and slow at first until she wrapped her arms around his neck, pulling him closer, and moaned softly into his mouth. Then it turned into something fast and hungry. They stopped only for a quick breath and locked lips again.

When Jade broke the kiss, her chest heaved against him as she panted for breath. "If skinny-dipping was this good when I was a teenager, I would have done it more often."

Lifting her off her feet, he wrapped her legs around his waist and pulled her against him, splashing water around them. His whole body tightened with the contact. Reflexively, he thrust his hips between her thighs, and she wiggled to get closer.

It was taking all his strength not to take things further. It didn't help matters when she rocked against him like she wanted him to do exactly what he was thinking. But he couldn't go there, not now. As much as it pained him to restrain himself, he didn't want their first time to be in the ocean like a couple of horny teenagers. Even though that's exactly how they were behaving.

But it wouldn't stop him from having *some* fun, and while Jade clung to him, Nate reached around her back and unclipped her bra. Sliding the straps down her arms, he let the bra fall into the water, and his hands immediately took its place. Her nipples peaked into hard beads, and he flicked and rubbed them, ripping a long moan from her. Then he replaced his hands with his mouth, sucking and licking as she gasped out his name.

Jade's hands did some exploring of their own and skimmed along his chest, down to his waist, and slid behind the elastic of his boxer briefs. His legs buckled as she clasped on to his arse, and he sucked in a sharp breath.

God, no matter how good Jade felt in his arms and how much he wanted her right now, or how fantastic it felt with her hands on his body, they needed to stop. Before they did something he told himself he wouldn't do. They were on a public beach. Even though it was late, anyone could walk past.

It almost killed him to pull away and set Jade back on her feet. She wobbled in the water and threw her arms around his neck to steady herself, plastering her wet skin against him. He was so tempted to slide his hands back onto her sweet breasts.

He wanted to continue, but someone needed to take control of the situation. And judging by the way she was nibbling at his neck, it wouldn't be Jade.

Before he could pull her away, a bright light coming from the shore shone in their direction. Jade squealed, darted a quick glance over her shoulder, and awkwardly waded through the water to hide behind him.

"You two out there. This is a public beach, and you're performing an indecent act. Get out of the water now."

"Connor, is that you?" Jade called.

"Jade?" the man shouted back. "What the hell are you doing? God, I already know... Christ, Jade. What were you thinking?"

"Someone you know?" Nate asked sarcastically.

Jade blew out a frustrated breath. "Yes, unfortunately. It's my older brother."

If there was ever a time Jade wanted the world to open up and swallow her, it was now. Too bad she wasn't a strong swimmer, because she would have kicked off and swam for New Zealand. Maybe she should try anyway and see how far she could get. Anything would be better than facing her police officer brother.

Thankfully, Nate's body was shielding her so Connor couldn't see her naked. That's definitely something she didn't need her big brother witnessing. God, how much did he see? She'd never be able to look him in the eye again.

"Jade Kathleen Brennan, get your arse out of the water now!" Connor shouted.

Jade groaned and thumped her head on Nate's back. "Kill me now please. All you need to do is hold my head under the water. One minute, two tops should do it." Then she grabbed Nate by the wrist, turned him around, and dropped his hand on top of her head. "Now push."

Nate chuckled and moved his hand under her chin and raised it. Water dripped off his hair and down his face. He took her breath away, and she almost forgot her brother was on the beach ready to taser them—*almost*.

"If I have to tell you again, I'm going to…going to…" Conner yelled.

"What, come in and get me?" She peeked around Nate's shoulder just in time to see Connor push his fingers through his hair and shake his head. "If you want me to come out, you need to leave."

"So you can continue what you were doing? Shit…the image is back in my brain."

She didn't have to wonder what he'd seen, probably a fair bit. Damn this full moon shining on them like a spotlight.

During the shouting between her and Connor, Nate hadn't said a word. Didn't even drown her like she'd asked. She looked at him and frowned. "Well…*do* something."

His eyes grew round. "What am I supposed to do? I'm worried if I say something, your brother might shoot me."

"Wuss. He's never shot anyone." She slapped him on the chest and let her hand linger for a beat. She'd really been enjoying feeling his firm body until she was rudely interrupted.

"I don't want him to start with me. He's busted his little sister naked in the arms of a stranger."

As if Connor could hear their quiet exchange, he yelled, "Who the hell are you with anyway? I'll lock him up for luring you here."

Nate's eyebrows lifted. "If only he knew *I'm* the inno-cent party, and his sister convinced me this was a good idea." He smiled with a gorgeous, crooked grin.

"I'm his sweet, little sister. He wouldn't believe it."

Nate looked unconvinced.

Then she called out, "Leave my friend out of this. We're coming out, but you'll need to turn around."

"Please don't tell me you're completely naked." Connor groaned.

"I've got undies on but…my bra floated away somewhere."

He swore like an overprotective brother, not an authoritative police officer.

"That was an expensive bra you lost," she said sternly to Nate.

"I can't say I'm sorry." His gaze was dark and hooded.

A tremor traveled through her body. But she mentally shook herself. Her brother was only a few meters away.

"Okay, I'm turning around," Connor said.

As much as she wanted to stay in the water and not face her brother, she knew she couldn't put it off any longer.

Peeking around Nate, Jade checked to make sure her brother had his back to them. "Okay, it's safe to leave."

"Safe?" Nate rubbed his chin.

"Well…he's not looking. What he'll do to us when we get out is anyone's guess."

"Let's get this over with." But Nate didn't sound eager to get out either.

They made their way to shore, and Connor kept his back to them as they put on their clothes. Because she was wet, Jade's dress clung to every curve and bump on her body. The smoldering gaze Nate shot her way told her she had a lot on display.

Connor didn't say a word to them as they did the walk of shame back to Jade's car. Probably so disappointed in her he couldn't find the words. Just like Mum used to do when they did something bad as kids. She'd scream over silly things, but when they'd done something worth yelling about, she'd go quiet, and that's when they knew they were in big trouble.

But Jade was a grown woman. Connor had no right to be mad. Although naked PDA wasn't exactly legal, and he was a police officer, so she could see why he was pissed.

At the car Jade turned to speak to Nate and found Connor standing shoulder to shoulder with him, pinning her with a disappointed look. She tilted her chin. No way was he going to make her feel like a kid in trouble. "Do you mind? I want to speak to Nate in private."

Connor turned toward Nate, giving him a once-over. By the expression on his face, it appeared he didn't like what he saw. Not much difference in height, Connor's head with his mop of coppery brown hair was just a little shorter than Nate's. But because of physical training to stay in shape for his job, her brother's build was bigger. Even though Nate had a good set of muscles on him too, she had a feeling Connor could take him on and win. And she hoped it didn't come to that.

"I'm staying here." Connor crossed thick arms over his chest.

Jade blew out a long, frustrated breath. "I swear to God, Connor, if you don't leave, I'll punch you."

"I'm staying, or I'll arrest you for public indecency, and if you punch me...assaulting a police officer."

She didn't believe him, but she was too tired to argue. "Fine! You are such a dick," she threw in to get the last word then turned her attention to Nate. His lips twitched. Yeah, this was so funny. "I'm sorry for my dip-shit brother." Connor made a huffing sound. "We didn't get to discuss the music program. I wanted to have it ready by the start of next week."

"Don't worry, I'll work something out. It will be fine. You get the kids there, and I'll get the music side done." He smiled and damn if it didn't make her knees knock together.

Even with her brother standing inches away, glaring at her, she knew she was definitely truly, madly, crazily in trouble.

Chapter 9

The next day, Jade drove to her mother's house and parked in the driveway next to Connor's jeep. She groaned. He was the last person she wanted to see. Last night had been the most embarrassing moment of her life. Well, it had started off great until the party pooper had to come and ruin everything. All she needed now was for Connor to blab to their mother about what happened.

"He better have kept his big mouth shut," she grumbled as she got out of the car.

As she entered the house, she could hear her mother and brother in the kitchen. She paused for a second and took a deep breath, squared her shoulders, and made her way down the hall. She wouldn't let Connor make her feel like a naughty child.

"Hi, Ma," Jade called out, walking into the kitchen.

When her mother turned around, her red curls

bounced around her disapproving face. Connor had spilled the beans. *What a jerk.*

"Jade Kathleen Brennan. Please tell me it's not true." Her mother frowned and put a hand on her curvy hip. She was shorter than Jade, but the way her disappointed crystal blue eyes bore into her, Jade felt two feet tall.

Jade threw Connor a dirty glare. His response was a smug smile as he leaned on the kitchen counter, crossed his legs at the ankles, and sipped from a mug.

"Depends on what you're talking about. If you want to know if I'm becoming a prima ballerina, well then no, it's not true."

Waving a finger at Jade, her mother's cheeks turned pink. "Don't try to be funny. What you did last night… I don't even want to think about it."

"Then don't. And Connor should mind his own business. He had no right blabbing it to you." She turned her attention back to her brother. "Are you five? Telling on me to Mummy."

"Oooh, are we talking about Jade skinny-dipping last night with some mystery guy?"

Jade whipped around to find her sister Kaitlin standing in the doorway.

Jade covered her face with her hands and shook her head. "Did you rat me out to everyone in the family? Should I be calling Granny in Dublin to see if she knows too?"

"There's a group email circulating as we speak," Connor said. When she dropped her hands and looked at him with what she hoped was pure evil, he only laughed.

"Kaitlin knows because I gave her a lift home after leaving you at your car. And Mum knows because she asked me if anything exciting happened on my shift last night."

"Oh, so you just *had* to tell her that I was skinny-dipping with Nate."

He shrugged, not looking sorry at all for the misery he'd caused her.

"I want to know *everything* about Nate. Give me all the details," Kaitlin said with a gleam in her eyes. "Or should I ask Connor to give them to me? I believe he said he had images he'll never forget burned into his brain." Her sister laughed when Connor scrubbed the palms of his hands over his eyes.

The weight of their questions on her shoulders made Jade drop on a chair at the dining table. "I'm not giving you details, and Connor couldn't have seen much because it was dark."

"Not that dark," he grumbled.

"Why would you do such a thing?" This from Jade's mother who sat at the opposite side of the table, frowning.

"I was helping Nate tick off things he never got to do as a teenager." And *she* got more than she bargained for.

"You did this as a teenager too?" Jade's mother's eyebrows disappeared into her hairline.

"Now you've put your foot in it." Connor chuckled.

"Only because I was with Kaitlin and she told me to."

Kaitlin gasped. "I only wanted to do it because I followed Connor one day and saw him with Penny from his year at school doing it and thought it looked like fun."

"What the hell!" Connor exploded and pushed from the counter. "Why were you following me?"

"You always told us to get lost. I wanted to see what you got up to when you snuck away."

"I told you to get lost *because* I didn't want you to see what I got up to."

Kaitlin tapped the side of her head and smiled sweetly. "Yeah. Well, I know a lot, so don't piss me off."

They were grown adults still squabbling like little kids. Jade watched her mother make the sign of the cross and look up at the ceiling, probably hoping for help from God for her children.

Connor shook his head. "I'm getting out of here. And you…" He pointed a finger at Jade. "Keep out of trouble. And if I find you doing something stupid like that again, I *will* arrest you." With that, he stormed out of the room.

"You'd think I robbed a bank or something. Skinny-dipping isn't that bad."

"Where did I go wrong?" Her mother sighed.

"So…who's this Nate guy you had sexy-time with?" Kaitlin's eyebrows wiggled as she asked.

"I don't think Ma wants to hear about it," Jade said as she looked at her mother.

"I've heard more than I'd like to, so I might as well know who my daughter's been fooling around with."

"We were just swimming," Jade lied.

Her mother arched an eyebrow. Jade mentally grimaced. It was mortifying to know her mother knew about last night.

Blowing out a long breath, she said, "As you know, his

name is Nate. He'll be teaching the kids music in our after-school program."

After a beat Kaitlin questioned, "That's it?"

"There's not much to tell."

"Oh, no way. You have got to give me more. How did you meet?"

"We met at a concert I went to with Liz." That was close enough to the truth, only omitting a few major details.

"*And...*" Kaitlin prompted.

"*And...*he happens to be friends with Toby, and they set it up."

Kaitlin narrowed her eyes. "How did you go from meeting at a concert to skinny-dipping?"

If she'd gotten arrested last night, she was sure she wouldn't have been interrogated like this.

"We've met a couple more times since the concert. Last night we had dinner to discuss the music program, and things moved on from there." Heat burned her cheeks as her mother watched her closely. "Can we drop it now please?"

"For now," Kaitlin answered. "But I'll have more questions when Ma's not around."

Jade's mother dropped her head in her hands. "I thought I raised good Catholic girls."

"We are, Ma." Their mother lifted her head and gave Kaitlin a skeptical look. "There's just a little devil on our shoulder that lets us have fun now and then."

This pulled a laugh from her. "This devil of yours must take after your father. Oh, that reminds me, he sent you a package. Probably for your birthday." She stood and headed out of the room.

"My birthday was a month ago," Jade said to her sister. Whenever her father was mentioned, an ache pressed against her chest.

"You're lucky, I waited two months for mine."

Their mother walked back into the room and handed Jade the package. Jade put it on the table.

"Aren't you going to open it?" her mother asked.

"I will when I get home."

Jade rose from the chair, gave her mother a kiss on the cheek, and tucked the package in her bag. "I'll see you next week." Then she gave a little wave to Kaitlin.

"I'll call you later. I'm dying to find out more about your new music teacher. I want to know if he's gorgeous and sexy." Her sister wiggled her eyebrows and laughed.

God help her. Nate was both of those things, and after getting a taste of him, how was she ever going to control herself around him now?

Later that evening, Nate sat on the couch in his rented house with sheet music scattered around him. Trying to find a song basic enough to teach young kids but one not so simple that it would put them to sleep.

Toby sat on a chair opposite him, eating chips from a bowl and watching the Flaming Stars football team play on TV. "Dammit, Lever dropped the ball!" he yelled. "That's the third time he's done that. Take him off!"

Being away so long, Nate didn't have much time to follow the local team and had no idea who Lever was. So he made the appropriate noises he thought Toby would want to hear.

As he narrowed his song choices down to five, his phone rang and he looked at the caller ID. It was his drummer Mike.

"Hey, man," he said as he answered the Facetime call and saw Mike's tired face. "It must be around five or six o'clock in the morning in New York. What are you doing up so early?"

"It's five, and I haven't gone to bed yet. Been at a gig with the boys and just rolled home."

"A gig?" They were on a break.

"Yeah, man, the boys were getting bored and itchin' to play, so we've gone to a couple of bars to jam. We've had Jimmy from Sonic Sound sing vocals. He just left his band and has been mucking around with us."

"Sounds like fun. He's got a good following. How's the response?"

"It's been good. Not as good as if you were playin' with us," Mike quickly added as if Nate might get offended that Jimmy was doing a better job. "When are you coming back? I know tour doesn't start for a few weeks, but I've got ideas for new songs I'd like to bounce off you."

A tightness clenched his stomach, and he ran his fingers through his hair. He wasn't ready. Not yet.

Nate had new songs of his own he'd like to work on, but he doubted Mike would want to add them to the band's playlist. "I have things I need to take care of here. I won't be back until maybe a week before we get back on the road." He glanced over at Toby who wasn't watching the football anymore but staring at him. "We'll have to work on them then."

Mike looked disappointed but said nothing more about it. "No worries. I'll email you what I've got so far. Check them out when you get time."

"Will do. Talk to you later." Nate ended the call.

Toby put the bowl of chips on the table. "You've only been on a break less than a week and they've replaced you? If you need to go back, I'm sure Jade will understand you can't do the music lessons."

Nate gave him a doubtful look.

Toby laughed. "No, she won't understand, but she'll get over it."

That he wasn't so sure of either.

"Seriously though, will you go back soon? Hearing they've gotten Jimmy to fill in for you can't be easy. He's a huge rock star."

"Are you saying I'm easily replaceable?" This was Nate's band. His father's legacy. No one could fill his shoes. So why did the possibility that someone might be able to hit him with a small amount of relief?

"No, mate, it wouldn't be easy. But stay away long enough, and with Jimmy filling in… Well, people can adjust to change quickly."

Trust Toby to give it to him straight, whether he wanted to hear it or not. "I'm only gone for a few weeks, then I'll be back on tour."

Toby nodded and dropped the subject. He pointed to the sheet music Nate had placed on the table. "All ready for your lessons? The parents are excited about the program. You'll have a full house."

Playing to a stadium of thousands of people was less nerve-wracking than the thought of teaching a room of primary school kids. What the hell had he gotten himself into? His palms began to sweat, and he rubbed them on the thighs of his jeans.

Toby continued, unaware of Nate's nerves. "Jade's gotten the room looking like a concert hall. She's more excited than the parents."

The thought of Jade's excitement brought him back to the night at the beach. She'd been excited then too, but for a whole different reason. He had to push the memory aside if he was to get any work done.

"I hope I don't let her down." If his voice sounded a little husky, Toby didn't notice.

"She wasn't happy with you the last time I saw you together. Have you kissed and made up since then?" Toby asked.

Nate made a choking sound. They'd done more than kiss, and it was safe to say after he had her naked in his arms, they'd made up.

Leaning forward in his chair, Toby placed his elbows on his knees. "Anything you'd like to share with the class?"

"Dude, you have got to get yourself out of the classroom from time to time," Nate said, trying to detract Toby from prying.

"Well, is there?" Toby looked at him like he was

talking to a sixth-grade student, knowing he was hiding something in his pockets. Did all teachers have that certain skill?

"Am I gonna get kicked out of school if I've messed around with the teacher?" Nate joked.

"Dammit, Nate. You can't fool around with Jade." Toby didn't find his joke funny.

"Why the hell not? Anyway, it's too late."

Toby's eyes narrowed. "Because she's too good for you. And why couldn't you keep your hands to yourself?"

Nate let out a harsh breath. "Well, thanks a lot," he said, not bothering to defend his actions with Jade.

Toby shook his head. "I didn't mean it like that."

"It sure the fuck sounded that way." But his friend was right, she was too good for him.

"If you start things with Jade, you're only going to leave, and that will cement in her brain even more that she's—"

"Cursed and will never find love. I know."

"She told you?" Toby asked.

"Yeah, and it's fucking ridiculous." Nate blew out a breath.

"We might think so, but she's dead set certain it's true, so don't get involved." Toby threw him a stern look.

"We only made out. I'm not offering her marriage."

"Good. It would be best if it didn't happen again. Just in case." Toby used his teacher's voice again.

There was no chance of Nate getting too involved. He was constantly on the move and relationships never worked. But having fun with Jade, knowing she wouldn't get attached because of the curse, was a win-win situation.

"What we do is none of your business."

Toby pinned him with a lethal glare. "If you hurt Jade, I will personally hunt you down and kick your arse."

Chapter 10

*A*s Nate walked into the school grounds, excitement rushed over him. Sure, he was eager to give the kids a music lesson, but it was seeing Jade again that put a smile on his face.

The last time they were together, she'd been dripping wet and seething mad. And he was glad he hadn't been on the receiving end of that temper. He also couldn't stop picturing the way her clothes had clung to her body.

As the kids rushed out of their classrooms after the end-of-the-day bell chimed, Nate knew he needed to get the erotic images of their teacher out of his mind.

He made his way to the hall. A group of kids who looked about six or seven were lined up at the door. Jade, with a clipboard in hand, was talking to them. He paused and watched the way she smiled and laughed at what the kids were saying. And the way they gave her their full attention. She definitely had Nate's attention too.

A heavy hand landed on his shoulder, and he turned

to find Toby. The corners of his mouth quirked like he knew something Nate didn't.

"I wouldn't blame you for being scared. A room full of six-year-old kids will not be easy." His friend laughed. "Good luck, buddy."

"You sticking around to watch the lesson?"

"No, I've got a meeting to get to. Have fun." Toby tapped him on the back and turned to walk away. Then he clicked his fingers and stopped. "Crap, I forgot my car has a flat battery. Do you mind if I take yours? If I'm not back after your lesson, Jade can take you home and I'll drop it off to you later."

"Sure." Nate dug the keys out of his pocket and tossed them to Toby. He caught them and waved goodbye.

Nate ambled over to Jade and the kids. When she saw him, she smiled but didn't quite make eye contact. A splash of pink colored her cheeks. Suddenly, the spitfire was a little bashful. She wasn't so shy when she'd pressed her naked body against him. God, if he continued to think of that night, he'd be dragging her somewhere private and there'd be no music lessons.

"Are you ready for class, Mr. Miller?" Jade's tone was formal.

"As ready as I'll ever be, Ms. Brennan." He mimicked her tone.

She gave him a half-smile, leaned closer, and whispered, "Don't let their innocent, little faces fool you. They can be devils."

The scent of flowers and sunshine drifted to him, and his nose flared at the enticing smell. *Damn the music lesson. Class is canceled.* But before he could grab hold of her and take her away, Jade was clapping to get the kids' attention.

"Children. This is Mr. Miller, and he'll be teaching you how to play musical instruments. Everyone, say good afternoon."

"Good afternoon, Mr. Miller," the kids said in a sing-song voice.

"Hey there, kids. I'm excited to get started. We've got great stuff for you to play with."

A tug at the leg of his jeans brought his attention down to a girl with straight, black hair and missing two front teeth.

"Do you do good lessons?" she asked with a slight lisp.

These kids were adorable. This shouldn't be too hard.

"Because my daddy said free lessons can't be good."

Well, adorable and honest.

"Megan, Mr. Miller is a very talented musician. The lessons will be amazing." Jade smiled apologetically at him. "Okay, quietly, and without running, go inside the hall and sit on the mat. Don't touch anything. We'll be there in a moment."

Once all the kids were inside, she turned to him, tucking a strand of curls behind her ear, and his gaze drifted to the smooth skin on her neck.

"Kids rarely have filters," she said.

Snapping his gaze back to her face, it took him a moment to understand what she was saying. "Don't worry, I've heard harsher words from adults."

She fiddled with more locks that had fallen from her bun and said, "Well, shall we start?"

Without waiting for an answer, she turned to follow the kids. But he held onto her wrist, stopping her. "Jade, are you okay?"

The way she fidgeted he'd think she was nervous. Was it because of the lesson, or did he cause it? With the way she avoided his gaze, he'd guess the latter. But why? Because of the night at the beach? Getting caught by her brother was probably embarrassing for her. For him it was damn inconvenient, but once he got his hard-on under control, he could see the funny side…barely.

"I'm fine," she said, her voice a little high. "If we don't go in now, the kids will attack the instruments even though I told them not to touch."

He didn't let her go, but instead pulled her closer to him. He didn't miss the sharp gasp and the way her gaze dropped to his lips. "That night at the beach—"

"Not now." Her head dropped, and she covered her face with her free hand. "I can't walk into the lesson with that on my mind."

Nate nodded, let go of her hand, followed her into the hall, and was smacked with the sound of rowdy kids.

***

From the moment Jade spotted Nate amble into the school grounds, memories from the beach flashed before her eyes. She didn't have to imagine what lay beneath his navy t-shirt and cargo pants he wore because she'd had her hands all over that fine body.

Now with him standing so close, she acted like a nervous schoolgirl. And when he put his hand on her arm, it sent a tingling sensation through her body. The move was far from seductive, but boy did it get her heart racing.

There was no way she could discuss what happened the other night right before a lesson. She couldn't look at all those sweet, little faces while her mind relived the most erotic moment of her life. Until Connor came along and ruined it. God, she'd never been so embarrassed. What must Nate think of her having a big brother scold her like a kid? Pathetic, that's what.

As they entered the hall, the noisy sound of children echoed through the room. It was too much to ask for them to sit quietly for a few minutes while the excitement and temptation of the instruments were displayed all around them.

She clapped her hands, and they stopped what they were doing and clapped the same rhythm back. Once they had quietened down, she asked them to sit on the mat.

"I'll let Mr. Miller take over the lesson now, but I'll still be in the room watching. So please listen to what he says." And she took a seat behind the class.

She watched Nate stand in front of the kids. He rubbed the palms of his hands on the front of his jeans. Wow, could a bunch of kids be making him nervous?

"As Ms. Brennan said, I'm Mr. Miller, but you can call me Nate. And I play guitar for…" Clearing his voice, he quickly amended, "I play guitar and a bunch of other instruments which I'll be showing you today. Hands up if you've heard of Jimi Hendrix." He glanced around the room, and when no one responded he asked, "What about Eric Clapton?" Again, nothing. "Eddie Van Halen, B.B. King?"

A few kids fidgeted and some yawned. Poor Nate, he looked disgusted that none of the kids knew these guitar greats.

Then Lachlan put up his hand, and Nate's face lit up, probably hoping there was one child who knew who he was talking about.

"When do we play the stuff?" Lachlan asked.

Nate's shoulders sagged for a beat. "Soon, buddy. Can anyone play a musical instrument?"

The whole class eagerly raised their hands. Jade hid a smile behind her hand. There was no way all these kids played. It was the reason she was having these lessons.

"Awesome. What can you play?" He pointed to Leon.

"All of them," Leon answered as he wiggled on the floor.

"Wow, that's impressive. Why don't you pick something and show me what you can do?" The skeptical expression on Nate's face showed he was on to him.

Leon bounded off the mat and picked the loudest instrument in the room, the drums. The shining kit a beacon to any little boy. He sat on the stool, picked up the sticks, and made a loud, horrible noise of banging and clanging.

Nate bit his quivering lip, trying not to laugh. He was

being polite, because Jade covered her ears. It was a good thing she sat behind the class so they didn't see her reaction and Leon was too involved in his drumming to notice.

Then all the kids stood up and shouted that they wanted to show him what they could play and ran to their chosen instruments. Within seconds, a chaotic amount of noise filled the room. Nate turned to Jade with a pleading expression. He had no idea how to control the little terrors. Laughter burst from her lips. Maybe starting with the youngest grade wasn't the greatest of ideas.

What the hell had he signed up for? No one warned him the kids would be out of control monsters. Sure, they looked so cute with their big, innocent eyes and missing teeth, but that was just a disguise. How did teachers deal with this every single day?

Nate watched Jade speak to the last parent to pick up their child. He overheard her saying, "It was a great lesson. They had so much fun. We can't wait to do it again next week."

None of what she said was true. It had been a train wreck. A disaster. Why bother telling them to come again next week?

Nate dropped onto the nearest chair, pushed his hands through his hair, and blew out a long, tired breath. All the muscles in his body ached like he'd done hours of weights, and a headache pounded in the back of his eyes.

He didn't have to keep doing this. If he hired someone to take over for him, everyone would be happy.

And then Jade turned around and smiled. His heart skidded to a stop. There was no way he could quit and let her down. How he'd make the lessons any better he didn't know, but he'd die trying, and dammit, those kids *would* learn to play. It would be worth the body aches and pains to see Jade smile at him like that again.

"You survived six-year-olds," she said as she took the seat next to him.

Survived just by the skin of his teeth. "Teachers are saints. To put up with so many kids at one time…" He shook his head. "I have no words."

Jade laughed. "You get used to it. It's not always so crazy. Once the excitement wears off, they'll behave better. You'll see."

"I'll believe it when I see it," he mumbled.

"You didn't like it?" she asked.

"I suck at teaching. You should look for someone else."

Jade's eyebrows rose. "You did not suck. I shouldn't have started you with such a young grade, but the kids had a blast, and you were great with them."

"Great? I'm not sure if you were in the same room. I didn't teach them a damn thing."

"Remember, they're only six. Unless they're musically gifted, learning an instrument will take time. Think about what went on in the lesson," Jade said.

"Nothing," he said. She narrowed her eyes, and he sighed. "They played around with the instruments."

"Exactly!"

"I'm not sure I'm following. Because what they did was make a lot of noise and couldn't follow any of my instructions," he noted.

"It wasn't about being able to play a song today. What they learned is what instruments they liked, what they were drawn to."

She was right. They didn't all gravitate to the same thing. And if something didn't feel right, they tried something else. By the end of the class, all the kids had chosen an instrument and had massive smiles on their faces. Jade had a point. They learned what they preferred to play. Hopefully, they could move on from there.

"I guess it can only get better, right?" *Please let it be so.*

Her eyes twinkled with laughter. "It will get better. I promise. And tomorrow you'll be teaching year five and six, and they'll be better behaved." She nudged him with a shoulder and smirked. "And maybe there'll be someone who'll know who Jimi Hendrix or Eric Clapton are."

Nate shook his head with disgust. "What are parents teaching kids these days?"

After locking up the hall, they made their way outside. "Toby's taken my car, and he messaged me to tell me he won't be back for a while. Do you mind giving me a lift home?" Nate asked. "If you can't, that's okay, I'll call a taxi."

Jade bit her lip. "I can give you a lift, but I'm not sure you'll want me to."

Confused, Nate asked, "Why wouldn't I? Are you

some kind of crazy driver that shouldn't be allowed on the roads?"

She gave him a sheepish grin. "I get called crazy, but it's not because of my driving."

Okay, now he was intrigued.

"Come with me. If you change your mind and don't want a lift, I'll understand," she said, and Nate followed her to the teacher's carpark. She probably drove an old bomb and was embarrassed.

When they reached the gravel lot, Nate stopped short. There wasn't an old bomb. Toby's car sat in the carpark and one other vehicle—a bright, canary yellow moped with matching sidecar.

"So, do you still want me to give you a lift home?" Her lips twitched.

Toby would've known all along what Jade drove to work that day. He was gonna pay for this. Could Nate even fit in that thing? And how safe could the tiny capsule be?

Jade pulled out a phone from her backpack. "I'll call Connor to pick you up."

God no. Not after the daggers the man gave him the other night, threatening bodily harm. How bad could a ride on a moped be? "It's fine. Just tell me how to get in it."

Jade gave him a dubious look. "Are you sure?"

Hell no, he wasn't sure. But he couldn't chicken out now. "Yes."

Unlocking a small compartment at the back of the vehicle, she pulled out two small black helmets and handed one to Nate. He inwardly groaned. It looked like something from an old world war two movie. If she handed him matching goggles, he was out of there.

With awkward movements, he got in, his knees almost touching his chin, and secured the belt nice and tight, making sure he wouldn't fall out.

She slid on the seat, adjusted her skirt, and tucked it under her legs, he assumed so it didn't flap around as she rode. When she started the engine, it sounded more like a lawnmower than any kind of motorbike he'd ever heard.

After giving her his address, he was hit with a thought. "Have you taken many people riding?"

She gave him a quick glance as she steered the bike out of the school. "You're my first. No one has been brave enough to try. Hang on!" She revved the throttle and took off up the street.

Nate clung onto the sides white-knuckle tight.

Chapter 11

*J*ade had laughed at Nate's shocked, white face when she told him she'd never taken anyone for a ride before. But the way he held on for dear life made her not feel so guilty for joking about him being her first passenger.

As they stopped in front of Nate's house, he fumbled with the seatbelt then jumped out of the sidecar. "Did you enjoy the ride?" she asked sweetly.

Something close to fear flashed in his eyes. Wow, he didn't have to look so terrified. It wasn't her fault a car pulled out in front of them and she had to slam on the brakes, nearly sending him flying across the road.

"No. Never again." He took off the helmet and threw it to her.

She caught it and was about to tell him to grow a pair when she saw a ginger cat sitting on the doorstep of the house. Like the animal knew it had drawn someone's attention, it meowed loudly. Jade looked closer and noticed its matted fur and skinny body.

Jumping off the moped and throwing the helmets in the compartment, she raced over to the cat. "Hey, sweet thing." Glancing over her shoulder, she asked, "Is he yours?" If it was, she'd blast him for neglecting the poor animal.

Nate shook his head. "Never seen it before."

"Are you lost? Looks like you haven't had a meal in a long time. I bet you're starving." In answer, the cat gave a long, pitiful meow. "We need to feed him," she said to Nate and tried to pick him up, but it scurried out of reach.

"*We* should leave it alone. It's a stray. Who knows what kind of diseases it has?"

Jade's brows drew together. "You'd let him starve?"

With a sigh, he said, "No." Then he pulled his keys from his pocket, unlocked the door, and entered the house. Jade followed, and so did the cat, like he knew food was close by.

Jade dropped her backpack on the floor near the door and gave the living room a quick scan.

"The kitchen's through there," Nate said, pointing. "Have a look at what you can find."

With that, Jade rushed out of the room. Inside the fridge, she found some roasted chicken. Pulling it out, she went in search of a plate and a bowl to pour water into. When Nate entered the kitchen, Jade had shredded the meat into small pieces onto a plate.

"Did you see how skinny he is? He probably hasn't eaten in days."

"Will the cat stick around because we're feeding it?" Nate asked.

Probably. "I'm sure he'll move on once he has a full belly."

Nate didn't look convinced.

She passed him the bowl of water and she picked up the chicken. "Let's feed this poor cat."

Jade had barely put the plate on the ground when the stray pounced on the meal, eating it at a fast speed. Then it attacked the water. When all was finished, it licked the plate and meowed, looking at Jade with eyes that said *please sir, I want some more.* Just like in the movie *Oliver.* How could she refuse that sweet face?

"I'll fix you another plate." Jade raced back to the kitchen to get more food.

Again, the cat devoured it super quick. This time, when he finished, he must've been content because he yawned, stretched, and found a spot under the coffee table and fell asleep.

When she looked at Nate, she found him smiling at her. "What?" she asked.

"Most people would have shooed the fleabag away. I know I would." He screwed up his nose as he stared at the cat. "If I have to fumigate for bugs, I'm sending you the bill."

"I couldn't let it starve, and neither could you." Making herself at home, she sat on the big, cushioned lounge, kicked off her shoes, and tucked her feet under her. "Spray insect repellent once he leaves. I'm sure it will be fine."

Nate sat down on the couch next to her. "I've never met a woman who rides a yellow moped and saves a kitten all in one day."

"I'm full of surprises." She grinned.

"I haven't had a dull moment since meeting you, that's for sure." His voice dropped to a huskier tone and his eyes hooded.

Her insides quivered, and a drumbeat banged against her chest. If he kept looking at her like she was dessert—wanting to lick and eat every last crumb—she'd let him take a bite.

So not to fall into temptation, she glanced around the sparse room. The only furniture was the couch they were sitting on, and a scarred timber coffee table that Dorito—yes, she'd named the cat—was sleeping under. A big, flat screen TV was mounted on the wall, and an old record player sat in the corner. There were no photos, artwork, or any personal touches.

"I'm loving your decorating skills," she commented sarcastically.

"No point doing more, it's only a rental. I'm never home long enough to buy anything."

"When was the last time you were home?" she asked.

He rubbed his chin. "Three years."

"Your grandmother must miss you when you're away. Do you have any other family here?"

"No, only Toby. We're not related, but he's like a brother."

She could tell Toby felt the same way about Nate. "What about family in America?"

"I'm an only child, my parents were too."

Jade thought how sad it was that Nate didn't have a lot of family in his life. She was lucky to have her grandparents, mother, siblings, and cousins constantly around. Even her father, although not as often, was present. She couldn't imagine not having them. Even when they stuck their noses into her business.

"I'm assuming being the only child of rich and famous parents, you would've inherited a fortune. How did you not turn out to be a spoiled rich kid?"

"Fi-Fi was my guardian and had control over the money. She made sure I couldn't touch it until I was mature enough to use it. And she often threatened that if I didn't behave, I'd never see it again. And whenever I tried my holier-than-thou bullshit, I'd cop a flick across the ear."

Jade chuckled. "She sounds tough. Although I think it was a smart move."

"She was. But she also gave me the love and affection I craved. I have her to thank for my great life living out of the shadow of celebrity parents."

"You don't use your parents' surname. Where did Miller come from?" Jade asked.

"It's Fi-Fi's maiden name. She kept it when she married my grandfather. He died when he was young, and no one ever figured out the connection."

What a crazy life Nate had led. After the trauma as a

young boy, Jade was happy he'd had somewhere safe and loving to land.

Her leg stiffened from having it folded under her, and she shifted on the couch to stretch. Nate took hold of her foot and placed it on his lap. Startled, she went to pull away, but he held tight and pressed his thumbs against the arch and gently massaged. Groaning, she slumped in her seat and closed her eyes. It felt like heaven.

His magical hands paused, and when he didn't continue, she cracked open an eye. If she thought he looked hungry for dessert earlier, she'd been wrong. Now he stared at her like she was three courses rolled into one. Heat coiled in her belly and simmered down to her toes.

The hands holding her foot slowly slid under her skirt and up to her calf, then he stopped, meeting her gaze like he was silently asking for permission to go further. God yes! Nothing would upset her more than if he stopped. And to show him her consent, her free foot glided up his thigh and ever so gently rubbed just below his arousal she could see straining behind his denim jeans.

He sucked in a sharp breath, and dropped his head for a beat. When he looked at her again, he said with a strained voice, "You know I'll be leaving in a few weeks."

Jade wiggled further down the couch to encourage Nate's fingers to slide even further up her leg. She would combust if he didn't put out this fire that was burning through her veins.

"So?" she managed to say on a frustrated sigh.

The hand holding her thigh wasn't doing what she wanted it to do, and she gave another encouraging wiggle.

"If we do this, it can't go any further. I'm only here for a few weeks. I can't commit to anything more," he explained.

Relationships in her life always had an expiry date. A tiny part of her wished things could be different with Nate. There was something about him that made her heart skip a beat like no one had ever done before. But she lived with the curse and knew the consequences.

"I'm okay with that," she said.

He gave her a wary glance. "Are you sure?"

"Yes, I'm sure. Are you always this chatty when you're about to have sex?"

He choked back a laugh. "Not usually. Just making sure we're on the same page."

Sitting up, she grabbed his shirt and pulled it over his head, tossing it on the floor. "You have nothing to worry about. I won't cry and chase after you when you leave." She flicked open the first two buttons of her blouse. "But if you think *you'll* get needy and clingy, then maybe we should stop?"

His eyes glazed over as he watched her fingers. "No chance of that happening." He growled and crushed his lips against hers, and they fell back onto the couch.

He made quick work of removing her shirt. For a second, Jade felt self-conscious about her less than ample chest. It was darker the other night in the water, and likely he hadn't noticed how lacking she was in that area. But when his mouth opened and sucked at her nipple through the bra, he made noises like he was enjoying himself, and all thoughts flittered out of her mind.

His tongue, wet and hot, was almost more than she could stand. But she *needed* more. More touching and more skin pressing against her. Her hands traveled down his back, clasping his butt and pulling him closer so he wedged between her thighs. The barrier of his pants getting in the way.

He pulled his mouth from her breast, and she nearly cried from the loss. As his heated gaze roamed over her body like a warm caress, she quivered. But she preferred the touchy-feely part a lot more and reached for the front of his jeans, unfastening the buttons of his fly. She wanted those suckers off—now.

Understanding her mission, he lifted slightly to give her better access, but when he glanced down to where their pelvises met, he chuckled. "Cute."

Who looked at a woman's lady bits and called it cute? Maybe love tunnel. Pathway to heaven. Pleasure purse. But cute? She took a peek to see what he thought was so *cute* then snorted. She was wearing her Powerpuff Girls undies. Well, that explained it.

"You are definitely unique." He chuckled.

"You can add 'awesome underwear wearer' to the 'moped rider and kitten rescuer' list."

He flashed her a smile, and she got back to removing his jeans. Not wanting to waste time, she roughly pushed them down, and his undies went with them.

But before they went any further Nate let out a loud scream and his face screwed up in pain. Then a startled cat screeched in fright and jumped off his butt. *How the hell did Dorito get there?*

Nate bounded from the couch, tripping over the tangled jeans around his ankles, and fell onto the coffee table, breaking through the flimsy timber.

Jade scrambled to her feet and gasped, "Are you okay?"

"The fucking cat clawed my arse!" he shouted.

Jade hid a giggle behind her hand.

"I'm going to kill it. Where'd he go?" He tried scrambling onto his feet but kept getting caught in his jeans.

"You're not touching a precious hair on Dorito's head," Jade scolded as she quickly put herself back together and then went in search of the cat. She found him shaking under a cushion that had fallen from the couch.

"What about the *precious* skin on my arse? Wait... you've named it Dorito?" This time he got safely to his feet, and much to Jade's disappointment, he pulled up his jeans, and then made to reach for the cat.

As if the animal knew his life was in danger and Jade was a safe place, he jumped into her arms. She held him close to her chest, trying to shield him from Nate. "Yes, I did. He's orange, skinny, and funny-looking. Just like a Dorito."

Nate shook his head with disbelief. "Well, I think *Dorito* has overstayed his welcome. Put him outside. After I disinfect my arse, we can get back to what we were doing. I'm interested in having a closer look at your special taste in undies." His eyes hooded, and her body quivered and she barely had any strength to hold on to the cat.

"Dorito stays."

"The fleabag goes. Would you like to see the razor-sharp cuts it left?" When her eyes sparked interest he said, "I'll show you a hell of a lot more if the stray leaves."

How could she pass that up? But to put the poor thing outside when it would need more food was too cruel. As her mind played tug-o-war, she heard her phone beep an incoming message. Carefully cradling Dorito, she walked to her backpack and pulled out her phone. It was an SOS from Ava. She was calling an emergency meeting.

"I have to go," Jade said.

"Right now?"

"Yes, my friend Ava needs me." She looked at Dorito, undecided what she would do with him.

"Here, give him to me."

She gave him a dubious look.

"I'll put him in the laundry room for the night."

"He'll need more food." She was still reluctant to let the cat go. Nate would probably toss him out the second she left.

"I promise I'll feed him and keep him inside. But tomorrow he's out."

She couldn't ask for more than that and couldn't force someone to take on an animal, especially when he wouldn't be around much longer to look after it.

She placed Dorito on the floor, and he scurried back under the couch pillow.

Nate grabbed her wrist and pulled her to him. "Do you really have to leave?"

Ava never sent an emergency message. Whatever it

was must be serious. But with Nate's body heat surrounding her and his warm breath tickling the sides of her neck, she was tempted to stay. It took all her willpower to push away.

"I'm sorry, I do. Can we make it another time?" She sounded like she was planning a lunch date, but inside she was shaking in her boots. She'd always been in a relationship when she had sex. Even though she knew it would eventually end, she liked having some kind of commitment first, even if it was only short-term. But Nate had her wanting him like she'd wanted no one before. And this time there wouldn't be any messy break-up drama. They both knew where they stood. *Winning!*

He pulled her back to him and gave her a curl-your-toes kind of kiss. It was so hot and sexy it surprised her she didn't melt into a puddle at his feet.

"We sure can. I'll see you tomorrow." His gravelly voice told her he was just as affected by the kiss.

She could only nod and float out of the house.

Jade and Lauren sat on Ava's black leather lounge and watched her pace, more like waddle, in front of the floor-to-ceiling glass windows that looked over Brimland Point beach. Since they'd arrived, Ava hadn't said a word, and it had been fifteen minutes.

Jade was getting worried. "Please, tell us—"

"I'm not ready yet." Ava stopped her pacing and held out her hand like a stop sign. Then waddled again.

Jade looked at Lauren. She only shrugged like she too didn't understand what was going on.

"I could've had sex with Nate by now." Jade flicked her wrist to check the time on her watch. "Will you be pacing much longer? Because maybe I can go back and—"

"You're sleeping with Nate?" Lauren gasped.

"My SOS interrupted sex?" Ava asked at the same time.

"No, I'm not sleeping with Nate…yet," she explained to Lauren. "And yes, you interrupted," she aimed at Ava.

"Wow, you've gotten hot and heavy fast with the sexy musician. You really are truly, madly, crazily in lust. That's my girl." Ava slowly sat down next to her and tapped Jade's knee. "Tell us how far you got, what you saw, and what you touched."

Jade laughed. "You're still such a perve. I thought married life would have sorted that out. And besides, we're here for *you*, not me."

"That can wait. Tell us," Ava encouraged.

"There's not a lot to tell, but there's definitely an attraction every time we see each other. And today I gave him a lift home after music lessons and things got a little heated, a cat attacked his arse, and then you called."

For a beat the girls stared wide-eyed with their mouths open. "A cat attack? Is this some new kinky move I haven't heard of? Because I've got every trick up my sleeve," Ava commented.

"No. We found a stray outside his house and… Never mind. It attacked and you messaged."

Ava shook her head. "Damn, my timing sucks."

Jade agreed. "Enough about me. Stop stalling, and tell us why we're here. And where is your husband?"

"I kicked Nick out." Ava sighed.

"What!" Jade and Lauren jerked straight-back in their seats.

Ava waved an arm. "Relax. I didn't kick him out permanently. I just needed space to figure things out."

Lauren held on to Ava's hand. "I thought your marriage was going strong. What's happened?"

"Calm down. We haven't broken up."

"Well, when you tell us you've kicked out your husband to figure things out what are we expected to think?" Lauren frowned.

"Maybe if you give me a chance to explain without interruptions, I'd tell you." Ava rolled her eyes.

Jade and Lauren both raised an eyebrow at their friend's sharp tone but kept quiet and waited for her to continue.

Ava took a deep breath. Her lip quivered, then she sobbed into her hands, "I'm having a baby!"

This was not new information. They'd known since the stick she'd peed on turned pink. And Ava's bulging belly was another clue. Seeing their strong friend break down over something she'd been excited about since she learned of the pregnancy was disconcerting.

"Yes, we know, but why is that bothering you now?" Jade rubbed soothing circles on Ava's back.

Ava pulled her shirt up to wipe the tears from under her eyes. God, even after a crying jag she still looked stunning. No blotchy or puffy eyes. If that was Jade, her face would have looked like she'd had an extreme allergic reaction to bees.

"I'm going to be a mother," she wailed.

Again, not new information. "We thought you were happy about this," Jade said.

"I am. But I don't know how to be one. I lost mine when I was young, and she wasn't exactly Mother of the Year. And what did she teach me when she was alive? When things got tough, drown everything out with vodka."

"Hey." Lauren got off the couch and kneeled in front of Ava to look directly at her face. "She may not have been a great mother, but she loved you. I had the worst mother in the world, and I'm doing a pretty good job raising Ryan. If I can do it, *you* can. You know what *not* to do. You'll be brilliant. And you have Nick, who will be an awesome dad."

Ava sniffed. "He will, won't he?"

"Absolutely. And you have us." Lauren pointed a finger between her and Jade. "And we will be phenomenal aunties."

This made Ava laugh, and she relaxed back in the seat. Jade knew she was only having pre-baby jitters and all would be fine.

It got her thinking how great her friends' lives had become. Both had successful careers. Ava was a partner in a law firm, and Lauren owned a gift shop and was doing interior design. Both were married to incredible men and were starting families. It was something Jade could never see in her future. Husbands and babies in her life would never go together. But she would love to one day have a child of her own. She didn't need a husband for that. Single women got pregnant all the time and could raise kids without a man.

With her mind made up she announced, "I've decided to freeze my eggs, and when the time's right, get a sperm donor."

Chapter 12

*T*he next afternoon, grades five and six kids raced out of the hall after class. Today's music lesson was a success. Not only did four children know some of the music greats, which put a huge smile on Nate's face, they could follow instructions and play basic notes to a song.

While Jade waited for Nate so she could lock up the hall, she pulled out her phone to check her messages. Lauren and Ava had texted her about the egg donor bombshell.

A text from Lauren read:

Jade, you need to seriously consider your options. Freezing your eggs and getting a sperm donor should be your last one. You don't have to have a baby on your own. Believe me, it's difficult. If I didn't have Jack, I don't know how I'd cope.

And this from Ava:

Making a baby in a Petri dish is too clinical and so not

sexy. Why don't you get Mr. Musician to help you out? In the fun 'let's get naked and sweaty' kind of way.

Jade laughed.

"What's so funny?" Nate said as he leaned over the back of her chair, his head inches away from her face.

Jumping, Jade almost dropped the phone on the floor. She swiveled in the chair to face him. "Oh, Ava thinks she's come up with a brilliant idea."

Nate raised a questioning eyebrow.

"I've been talking to the girls about having a baby, and I'm considering freezing my eggs and using a sperm donor when I'm ready. But Ava thinks I should use you."

"What the hell?" Nate straightened and took about one hundred steps back—okay, maybe only two, but his reaction was hilarious.

"Relax. She was only joking… Well, I think she was. With Ava you can never tell. Don't worry, I'd never ask you to be a donor. Unless you wanted to. Do you want to?"

Nate stood rock solid. Speechless.

Jade burst out laughing, clutching her stomach. "If you could see the look on your face. Scared much?"

Grabbing her hand, he pulled her onto her feet and wrapped an arm around her waist, crushing her chest against his. He ran the pad of his finger along her collarbone. The fingertip glided down the V of her top and back up again. The laughter died instantly, and Jade bit her bottom lip.

"If you could see the look on your face. Turned on much?"

This time it was Nate's turn to laugh, but it was soon cut off when Jade slid her hand over his arse and squeezed. "I sure am." No point denying it.

He grinned slow and sexy. "Let's get out of here."

"I wish I could, but I have a meeting in about ten minutes." Jade sighed.

"Another meeting? Is your friend okay?"

"This is a parent-teacher interview for one of my students. And yes, Ava's good. She's pregnant and had pre-baby jitters."

"What about tonight?"

"I meet the girls every Tuesday night at Jovi's for drinks. It's a ritual we never miss unless there are dire circumstances."

The golden flecks in his hazel eyes flashed liquid heat. "I can think of something *dire* that's making me extremely uncomfortable at the moment. Are you sure you can't miss it?"

Her gaze dropped to his crotch for a beat. Yep, there was no mistaking his discomfort. "Sorry, we never put guys before girls."

Stepping away, her body already missed his closeness and heat, but she really had to go. She picked up her bag, and they walked out of the hall, locking the door behind them.

Then she remembered the cat. "How's Dorito?"

"Full and happy. I put him outside this morning, and I haven't seen him since."

"You didn't keep him?" What was she saying? She already knew he couldn't.

He frowned. "I'm not staying long enough to have a pet."

The thought of him leaving left her with a heavy heart. It was probably because they'd become friends—hopefully, friends with benefits. And a man so gorgeous would make any woman sad to see him go. The weight on her chest couldn't be for any other reason.

———

A scrawny ginger cat sat at his doorstep when Nate arrived home. "I knew if I fed Dorito, he would only keep coming back," Nate grumbled.

He walked up the two front steps and frowned. Christ, now Jade had him calling it by name.

Big copper eyes stared back as he dug the keys out of his pocket. Dorito wound his body around Nate's legs and meowed.

"If you think you can sweet-talk me into letting you inside for more food, you are mistaken big time, buddy. You don't have a sexy redhead here to help you out this time."

Once he had the door unlocked, he didn't open it fully. He squeezed himself through the small gap so the cat couldn't squirm his way in, and quickly shut the door behind him.

"Surely he'll find another sucker to feed him."

After a quick shower, Nate went into the kitchen to see what he could put together for dinner. When he opened the fridge, he smiled. Fi-Fi had come over sometime during the day and left him a tray of lasagna. But what had made him smile was a note she'd left propped on the dish.

There's enough for two. Maybe you'd like to share it with your cute teacher. Enjoy.
      Love, Fi-Fi.

Nate knew his grandmother would have done some research on Jade. Fi-Fi could be like the FBI and probably had a file thick with information. He shook his head. She meant well. She wanted to see him settled down and happy.

After cutting a slice of lasagna, he heated the meal in the microwave. When it was done, he took the plate to the living room and set it on the couch—the coffee table now firewood. He pulled out an old Cold Revenge vinyl and put it on the record player he'd pulled out of the garage of his grandmother's house. The rough and raw sounds of electric guitar, bass, and drums filled the room; sounds that as much as Nate tried to emulate, he could never achieve. His dad was a genius in his craft.

As he listened to the scratchy sounds of vinyl—the way music should sound in his opinion—an unmistakable meowing noise came from the front door. *Dorito.*

Nate turned the volume up to drown out the sound, but as he went to fork a bite of food into his mouth, the meowing only grew louder. Like the cat knew he had to compete with the music.

Sighing, Nate dropped the fork back on the plate. If Jade found out he ignored the stray, she'd be spitting mad and he'd never hear the end of it. He got off the couch, marched to the door, and swung it open. The cat darted in the house like the Flash, jumped on the couch, and scoffed into his pasta.

"Hey! That was my piece."

There was no chance Dorito was giving up his feast, and Nate had no intention of fighting for it. Going back to the kitchen, he heated another plate of food and ate it standing up. He didn't want to take any chances of the cat stealing more.

Back in the living room, Dorito had finished his meal and curled up in a corner of the couch, purring like a freight train. He was one content feline and didn't look like he was going anywhere soon.

Nate left him alone, turned off the record player, and went to work on the songs Mike had emailed him. It was too late to call him in New York to discuss them, so Nate grabbed his laptop from his bedroom and sat gently on the couch next to Dorito, trying not to disturb him. *What the hell!* He was worried about waking the fleabag now?

Opening his laptop, he pulled up the email. You'd think he'd just opened a can of tuna because Dorito's eyes flew open. He stretched, pushed himself under Nate's arm, and made himself comfortable on his lap. The cat closed his eyes, tucked his face under a paw, and the loud purring started again.

For a moment Nate sat stunned with his computer sitting precariously on his knees. How was he supposed to work with this bag of bones on his lap?

He nudged him with a finger. "Move."

Dorito didn't bat an eye.

He poked again, this time harder. "I said move."

No response. As soon as the cat woke up, he was going back outside. And Nate would never feed him again, no matter how loud he meowed.

He shifted so he could reach the keys on the computer and scrolled through Mike's email. Listed were five new song titles with lyrics. "He's been busy."

He skimmed through them, making notes of what he liked and what needed fixing. Then he opened the video Mike also sent. He'd titled the song *Stop Calling*. Nate watched his drummer and guitarist perform. It was good. Edgy and heavy on guitar. The fans would love it. Much like his father's music, it had all the rough sounds of a heavy rock band.

"Why don't *I* love it?" He rubbed the back of his neck. He'd grown up listening to this style, was taught it the second he was big enough to hold a guitar. The son of Liam Harvey had his father's passion passed down to him.

Maybe it was too soon after the tour to appreciate what Mike had sent. He was tired. Months of non-stop touring and living two different lives had drained him. He needed the break to recoup and focus on the band and make new music.

He didn't bother opening any other videos. Instead, his gaze drifted to the guitar leaning against the wall. A strong pull to pick it up and play made him gently shift Dorito and move him on the couch. One eye cracked open to give Nate a dirty look, and then he rolled into a ball.

Nate put the computer on the floor and walked over to his six-string. The manager at Jovi's said he could play there whenever he wanted. And if that wasn't motivation enough, Jade said she would be there. With that, he picked up the guitar, flung the strap over his shoulder so it sat on his back, and was about to leave the house when he stopped short. He had to put Dorito outside.

Turning back, he looked at the scruffy pile of ginger hair fast asleep on the couch and didn't have the heart to kick him out onto the street. He'd deal with him in the morning, and if he kept coming back, maybe he could find him a more permanent home.

Happy with his decision, he left the house.

Chapter 13

A light summer drizzle fell as Jade ran from her car to Jovi's Pub, damning the frizz that the rain was doing to her hair. Under the pub's awning, she tried to smooth it out with her hands but eventually gave up and pushed through the timber doors.

Immediately, she heard a voice she would recognize anywhere. Not Nathan Harvey, the grungy, edgy style that sang for Harvey's Territory. It was the smooth, crooning voice of the ever so sexy pub singer, primary school music teacher, and the man she was truly, madly, crazily in lust with—Nate Miller.

It didn't take him long to spot her. Probably because she was so entranced by the music and the hot singer, she'd bumped into a table and empty glasses toppled over, causing a crashing sound loud enough to echo through the room. Because of the ruckus she'd made, she received a few dirty looks from people sitting at nearby tables. She smiled apologetically and then made her way to where Lauren and Ava sat.

"You sure know how to make an entrance," Ava whispered.

"The table jumped in front of me," Jade said as she took a seat between them.

Ava rolled her eyes and laughed.

"Shhh." This came from Lauren. "I want to listen. He's so good."

Ignoring her friend, although Jade agreed one hundred percent, she leaned toward Ava and said, "I don't know if I should be happy to see him here or annoyed. I told him we couldn't meet tonight because I was having drinks with you girls. And now here he is."

"Honey, if that man is here to see you, I'd be happy. And I mean *happy* in all the right places." Then she sighed and rubbed her belly. "I can't wait until this baby is born so I can get back to being happy in all the right places."

Jade sniggered.

Lauren glared at them and held a finger up to her lips, signaling for them to be quiet. That only made Jade and Ava laugh even more. Lauren shook her head and continued to watch Nate.

Until now, Jade had avoided looking at him. Afraid that if she did, she'd run to the stage and throw her bra at his feet with her phone number on it. But luckily for her, he'd already seen her bra and had her phone number. So maybe it was safe to have a quick peek.

She turned her head, and *bam*, the sight hit her like a blow to the chest. A black t-shirt hugged his broad chest, and he wore faded denim jeans. A lock of dark sandy hair fell over his forehead as he sat on a stool strumming his guitar. Tonight, he sang something about trailing his fingertips down his lover's spine.

It made her own spine tingle and her heart race. Her palms grew sweaty, and she was short of breath. Maybe she was coming down with something and needed medical attention. Or maybe she just needed Nate doing all those things he sang about to *her*. She squirmed in her seat.

Finally, when he finished the last notes of the song, he leaned the guitar against the stool and gave a little wave to the audience who rose to their feet as they applauded.

"Wow, he's fantastic." Lauren clapped enthusiastically then turned in her seat to give them her attention after going fangirl over Nate. "Why haven't I seen his albums anywhere? Surely someone would want to sign him up."

Keeping who he really was from her friends was the worst. Actually, not being naked right now with Nate was the worst, but keeping secrets came close. She wished she could tell them.

After his set, Jade hoped Nate would come over to say hi, but he walked to the bar and ordered a drink. She watched him pull back on his beer, not giving her any attention at all. She looked away. Maybe he didn't want to interrupt her while she was out with her friends.

Should she go to him and say hi? God, she felt like she was back in high school trying to pluck up the courage to talk to the hottest guy in class. They'd gotten to know each other pretty intimately, so why was she suddenly feeling so shy? Then a tingling sensation along her spine pulled her gaze to his face. His hooded stare locked onto hers, and she flushed red hot.

"It's seriously getting hot in here. Don't you think, Lauren?" Ava said, waving a hand in front of her face. "If you don't go over there and drag that man away, I will do it for you."

Jade broke eye contact with Nate and lifted a dubious brow at Ava. "Really?" There was no way in hell she would cheat on her husband. And if she did so with Nate, Jade would strangle her.

"No. One man in my life is more than enough," Ava replied.

Once upon a time, Ava never wanted only one man. Didn't believe in relationships. Now, Jade had never seen her friend looking so happy. How things can change.

Things can change... Could they for her too?

She mentally shook her head. The curse situation was out of her hands. No point getting her hopes up. Disappointment sat heavy on her heart, but she shrugged it away. She may not be able to plan a future with a man, but nothing stopped her from having a lot of fun with one. And Nate had come-and-have-fun-with-me written all over him.

"Sorry, girls, but I'm cutting our night short," she said as she rose from the seat.

"About time." Ava cheered.

With that, Jade gave her friends a quick kiss on their cheeks and headed toward Nate with the thundering of her heart beating like a drum in her ears.

She slid onto the stool next to him. "I've changed my mind. I've decided tonight it's guys before girls."

———

Nate should have felt guilty Jade ditched her friends for him. Wasn't there some kind of code about friends that shouldn't be broken? But if she was okay with it, why the hell should he feel bad? From the moment she stumbled into the pub he wanted to stop singing and take her somewhere private so he could do all those things he'd been fantasizing about for days.

And when she'd approached him, it took all of two seconds to usher her out of the room. Once outside, he remembered he'd walked. His house was only a block away, but it was now raining hard.

"I don't have my car." Standing under the awning, he asked, "please don't tell me you came here on your little bumble bee."

Placing a hand on her hip, she feigned being offended. "My moped is excellent transportation, but no, I brought my car because I knew it would rain." She lifted a lock of hair and examined it. "I got stuck in the rain anyway, and look at the mess it made of my hair."

Nate took the strand from her hand and twirled it around his finger, gently tugging her head closer to him so their faces were inches away. Her sparkling, light blue eyes deepened, and her tongue darted out to lick her bottom lip, drawing his gaze to her mouth.

Oh God, that mouth. He wanted to taste her again so

badly. But he had to restrain himself. Because if he kissed her now, he wasn't sure he'd be able to stop, and having Jade up against a wall in front of a busy pub was not the way he wanted her.

"Let's get out of here." His voice sounded husky. He held onto her hand and they darted out into the rain. "Which way?"

She pointed left, and they ran about six meters down the road. Both of them were soaked through when they jumped into the car. Nate made out the lace pattern of Jade's bra under her pink top. Her nipples peeked.

Inwardly, he groaned. He'd been a teenager the last time a glimpse of a girl's bra had turned him on. Now he'd seen his fair share. Women constantly flashed them, and much more, at his concerts. But it was only Jade's he wanted to see. The sooner the better.

"Your place or mine?" she asked, her voice sounding a little breathless. He hoped it was because of him and not from the jog to the car.

"My place is two minutes away. How far is yours?" he asked.

"Too far. Your place it is." And she preceded to get them there in under two minutes. Thank God her car was faster than her moped.

Arriving at his house, they entered the living room and were greeted by the cat sitting beside the door like he was waiting for them.

"Dorito!" Jade smiled and kneeled on the floor. "How are you, baby? Did you miss me? Has Nate been good to you? He'd better be." She spoke to the cat like he could understand her.

The cat rubbed up against her legs, something Nate wanted to do and would not be outdone by it.

He pulled Jade up onto her feet and led the way to his bedroom. She followed close behind and so did Dorito. "No, you don't, buddy. The only claw marks I want on my arse tonight are from Jade."

Jade snorted but didn't complain when he gently pushed the cat out of the room and closed the door.

For a moment all Nate could do was stare. Her flaming hot hair sat in wild, damp curls, framing her round face. The freckles on her nose stood out against her fair skin. She might not like them and tried covering them up, but he thought they were sexy as hell.

His heart was in his throat as he took in the rest of her. Her wet top stuck to her like a second skin, showcasing everything he wanted to touch. She was gorgeous. She made his mouth water and his pulse beat fast.

He reached for her, but she held out her hand to stop him. "Wait, we need to talk."

Christ! She wanted to talk *now*? "Can we talk while we're taking our clothes off?" He reached for her again, but she stepped out of his way. He blew out a frustrated breath and dropped onto the edge of the bed. "What do you want to talk about?"

"I know we mentioned this before, but I just want to double check that we're still on the same page. You're leaving and going back on tour?"

Nate nodded. Although the thrill of tour had died a long time ago, he knew it was where he needed to be.

"And I'm cursed, so there is no chance I'll get attached and have you break my heart when you leave. It's obvious I have the mega hots for you, but I will *not* fall in love."

That curse was absolute bullshit. One day some guy would convince her of it, and she'd fall madly in love and have the happy relationship she deserved. An urge to punch that phantom man was strong.

She continued, unaware of the anger for her future boyfriend bubbling in his gut. "So as long as you keep to your part of the deal and go back on tour, forming no attachments, I'll keep to mine." She held out her hand. "Do we have a deal?"

He grabbed it and pulled her down. She squealed as she fell on him. Then he rolled them so she was on her back and him on top. He trailed his lips along her smooth neck, nipping with his teeth at her racing pulse. "Freckles, we have a deal."

Chapter 14

*J*ade let out a long, needy moan as Nate continued kissing her neck and a hand went exploring her breasts. Hopefully, they would be naked soon, with Nate between her thighs. She could hardly wait. But for now, she enjoyed Nate's magic fingers as he tugged and flicked her nipples through the thin fabric of her top.

Wanting to do some exploring of her own, she pushed her hands between their joined bodies and slid them down his firm chest. The man had steel behind his shirt. She grabbed his shirt and pulled it over his head, placing slow kisses along his chest.

He groaned as he tunneled desperate fingers through her hair, pulling her lips to his and sweeping his tongue in her mouth. She shivered.

"Are you cold? It's probably your wet clothes. I should take them off for you," he said with a sinful smile.

"I'm glad you're looking out for my health." She giggled.

In a flash, her clothes were off and thrown all over the room. All she was left in was her bra and undies. Nate looked down at her undies, threw his head back, and laughed. This was the second time he'd laughed at her vagina; she'd start to get a complex.

"Thor undies? They make this stuff for grown arsed women?" His eyes sparkled with mirth.

"Yes, they do, and I happen to be a fan of superheros, especially Thor's powerful hammer." Her lips twitched.

Nate's gaze traveled down her body, sending sparks of lightning through her veins. Desire sizzled in all her good spots. She could only imagine the way she was looking back at him. Like he was a giant Krispy Kreme donut she wanted to lick all the icing off of first before taking a huge bite. But in a sexier kind of way.

Putting his mouth to her ear, he whispered, "I have a hammer more powerful than Thor's."

She trembled. "Maybe you're all talk?"

"Freckles, I'm about to show you," he promised as he licked and sucked her neck while his hand massaged her breast.

Arching her back off the bed, a long moan escaped her lips, and she slid her hands down his strong back, clinging onto his butt to pull him closer to where they were joined. She rocked against him; she needed to feel more of him. Wanted him inside her. The denim jeans he wore were a barrier against her happy place, and they needed to be removed.

She reached the front of his pants, popped open the buttons, and slid her hands inside the waistband. Wowza! He was going commando. Just one more thing to heat her body.

As she reached what was so obviously happy to see her, Nate's head dropped to her shoulder, and he sucked in a low breath. She nibbled and licked his shoulder—so much tastier than a donut—as he ground into her hand.

But there was still the problem with the jeans on his body and him not being inside her, so she pushed them as far as she could down his legs. When he stood to pull them all the way off, she got an eyeful of a beautiful man. This guy was better than Thor, and his mighty hammer was more impressive.

He gazed down at her like she was the most gorgeous woman in the world. A girl could get used to being looked at like that.

No, this is temporary. But I'll take it while it's hot.

She slid her hands down her body, slipped her fingers into the waistband of her undies, and tugged them off. Nate stood as still as stone. Then she rose to her knees, reached behind her back, unclipped her bra, and let it fall off.

For a beat he closed his eyes and swallowed hard then left the room.

What the hell? She'd gone all-sexy-striptease mode and he left!

Before she could bound off the bed and follow to demand answers, he walked back in carrying a box of condoms. She'd been so turned on, protection hadn't crossed her mind. Thankfully, Nate was better prepared.

"We need a whole box?" Her voice shook.

He chuckled low and sexy. "I'm up for it if you are."

The challenging words vibrated through her, sending liquid fire through her veins, and her eyes dropped to exactly what was *up*. "I'm game," she said and laid back on the bed.

This time there was no laughter in his eyes. Only heat and a promise of a sinful night shone through them.

He took the foil packet out of the box and ripped it open, rolled it onto his erection, and joined her on the bed. She whimpered as he settled himself between her legs, and she wrapped them around him, encouraging him to take the next step. And thank God, he took the hint. As he kissed her long and deep, with so much passion, he slowly slid into her. She sighed, moaned, whimpered. It was that *good*.

And he made his fair share of noises too. Cursing as he entered and hissing low and raspy when he moved.

Her hands got busy gliding over his shoulders, down his back, and onto his butt. His mouth got busy kissing her lips, neck, and then her breasts. A jolt of electricity flashed through her body as he sucked a nipple into his mouth, leaving her squirming and breathless.

Nate rocked harder, faster, and heat boiled inside her. She wrapped her legs tighter around him, pulling him closer. Wanting their bodies so close they'd need the Jaws of Life to pull them apart.

And when her body couldn't take any more, she

exploded into a magnitude of feelings and sensations. Stronger than anything she'd ever felt before. A moment later, Nate was right along with her as they both fell apart.

When Jade came up for air, the only words she could string together were, "Holy crap balls!" as she lay panting and quivering beneath Nate.

Nate laughed, the vibrations trembling through her body and his warm breath tickling her neck. And just like that, she was turned on again.

"You're a musician, right? I'm hoping encores aren't only for the stage."

He shifted and leaned on an elbow, his hair falling over his forehead. The need to push it away felt a little too intimate even after they'd been as close as two people could get. Touching him that way was more of a lover's touch, not from someone temporary.

"I do encores only when the crowd cheers loud enough." He gave her a lopsided grin. "I need to hear you scream."

"Oh, honey." She rolled over and straddled him. "By the time I'm finished, *you'll* be the one screaming for more."

Something warm and smooth snuggled against Nate's side. He cracked open sleepy eyes then smiled as he looked at Jade. Her arm was flung across his chest, and her leg was tangled with his. Her red, curly hair fanned out over the pillow. A tug pulled at his chest. She was beautiful inside and out. It would be tough letting her go.

Slowly, she stirred, stretched, and looked around the room. Like she just realized where she was, her eyes widened and she attempted to sit up, but he stroked a hand down her back and secured it around her waist, not ready for her to leave yet.

Flicking a quick glance at the clock on the bedside table, she said, "It's getting late. I should go." But she made no more attempts at getting out of bed.

Her voice was low and husky from sleep, and damn how it caused his blood to head south between his legs. After giving her three orgasms, he should let her rest —for now.

To distract himself, he said, "Tell me about this family curse."

She stiffened, so he trailed his fingers along the curve of her hip, and she softened against him again. "I've already told you a witch—"

"Yes, a witch put a curse on your family. But why?"

He didn't believe in witches and curses, but it was something that played heavily in Jade's life. There must be a reason, a *real* reason, why she'd cling onto such a farfetched story.

She chewed on her bottom lip then said, "When I was about ten, my family took a trip to Ireland to visit my grandparents. They had a room filled with antique furniture, paintings, and books, and I spent hours in there looking at all the stuff. One day, I found an old diary written by my great-great-great grandmother. In it she wrote how her son was cursed by the town's healer."

"What did he do? And I thought a witch cursed him?"

"My grandmother's son got the healer's daughter pregnant while he was engaged to another woman. And instead of ending the engagement and marrying her daughter so their child would be legitimate, he went ahead and married his fiancée. After she put a curse on him, the town started calling her a witch."

"A baby born out of wedlock would have been a big scandal back in those days," he said.

"You're right. It was a small village too, so they all knew everybody's business. The healer's daughter became an outcast. No one would hire her for anything. No one wanted to marry a woman carrying another man's baby. And to make my great-great-grandfather pay for ruining her daughter's life, she put a curse on him so he would know what it was like to feel the heartache of any daughter he had losing the love of her life. So, in the future, all women who are fathered by a Brennan man will never find true love. The men they want will always leave them, and they'll be left heartbroken."

He took a moment to process the story. The imagination of a ten-year-old girl reading an old diary could spin into overdrive. "Do you know how many women have had failed relationships?"

Her brow furrowed, and she squinted her eyes like she was thinking back. "Well, only the women I've known. My parents divorced when I was young." A flash of pain shot from her eyes.

"Divorce is tough on kids," he said.

But she shrugged like it had been no big deal.

"And you believe the curse did it?"

She threw him a look as if to say *haven't you been listening to a word I've said?* "Yes, it did. Why else would my dad leave his family?"

Nate could think of many reasons, some men were arseholes, but he kept his opinion to himself. "You don't see him anymore?"

She threaded the edge of the sheets through her fingers. "He's a pilot and is away a lot, He visits when he can." At her clipped tone, he could tell talking about her father was a touchy subject, so he dropped it.

"Who else has experienced the curse?"

"My sister Kaitlin is also divorced. It only lasted six months. Liz was about to get married, but he ran off before the ceremony. My grandfather died."

"Wait… This curse causes death too?" He lifted onto an elbow.

"He's been the only one."

"How old was he?"

"Eighty-one," she answered.

"Did your grandparents stay married until he died?"

"Yes." She blinked with surprise like it had only just occurred to her that there was a relationship that had lasted.

He raised an eyebrow. "Then it didn't curse everyone."

"I guess not, but their relationship wasn't a loving one."

"But it *lasted*. Your grandfather never left your grandmother. Maybe this curse is just an old wives' tale." No *maybe* about it. "And relationships can last."

She pushed away from him and sat up. "That's just one amongst hundreds."

"Hundreds? These men had to last a while in relationships to have hundreds of ancestors to have this curse continue to the present day. Or did they go around getting every woman they met pregnant?"

She bounded off the bed, dragging the sheet with her and holding it to her chest to cover her naked body. He inwardly sighed. Roadblock. There would be no more sex tonight. Or ever. Why didn't he just agree with her and shut his big mouth?

"Jade, I'm sorry."

He reached out a hand to pull her back into bed. She turned her nose up at it and went searching for her clothes. What she didn't know was that while she covered her front with the sheet, her back was bare-arsed naked. And he was getting the best view in the house.

He leaned back on the headboard and placed his hands behind his head. Damn, she looked amazing. Even with her flaming hot temper.

When she glanced over her shoulder, following the direction of his gaze, she squealed and wrapped the sheet around her whole body, throwing him a dirty look.

He shrugged. "Can't blame a guy for looking."

That earned him an eye roll.

"Jade, come back to bed."

With her clothes held to her chest, trying to keep the sheet in place, she sighed. "I'm always getting teased. It would be nice if *one* person, especially the one I just bumped bodies with, took me seriously."

Well, now he felt like shit for upsetting her. "It's not every day you hear about witches and curses." He rubbed a hand along his jaw. "Stranger things have happened in the world. I've always tried to be open-minded, and I will about this too."

It was all he could come up with without pissing her off again. And for now, it was for the best Jade believed in the curse. Because whatever was going on between them couldn't go past the bedroom. He couldn't offer her more.

One day she'd stop believing in the curse because she'd love some lucky bastard who fought hard enough to stay. Unfortunately, it couldn't be him.

"Come back to bed," he said again. "I'll make it worth your while."

A line appeared between her brow as she bit her lip. "Because you're only here for a few weeks, we *should* make the most of it. Not argue. It would be a shame to go home now." The clothes she held dropped to the floor.

"A big shame. But you know what can be better than sex?" he asked.

Jade raised an eyebrow.

Grabbing the sheet still wrapped around her, he tugged her onto the bed. "Make-up sex."

She laughed as he rolled on top of her. "I've never had make-up sex before."

"Freckles, you're in for a treat."

Chapter 15

*J*ade listened to the year three and four students practicing the first verse of *Wanted Dead or Alive* Nate had taught them. With his patient instructions, they'd picked it up quickly. He had a knack for keeping the kids entertained and interested in music. And they adored him. Who wouldn't? He was a rock god, and it showed in the way he moved, played, and sang. And he made every one of those kids believe they could be just like him if they kept practicing.

But her gaze wouldn't stay focused on the students; it kept getting drawn to the music man strumming his guitar. She watched the way he caressed the strings, and flashbacks from the night before played in her mind. Those callused fingers got her singing a sweet tune too. She crossed her legs and fanned her face with a notepad. Was it getting hot in here?

Then, as if Nate could read her dirty mind, he pierced

her with a sizzling look and winked. The kids stopped playing and laughed.

"Okay, guys and gals. You're sounding pretty amazing. And because you've picked up that verse super-fast, we'll learn the chorus next lesson." They all smiled at the compliment. "Put your equipment away, and I'll see you next week."

As soon as the last student left the hall with a parent, Nate came from behind her and wrapped his arms around her waist. "I didn't hear you leave this morning."

She was glad for his support, because the feather-light kisses he was gliding up and down her neck were turning her knees to jelly. She'd been tempted to wake him up with a good-morning quickie. But she knew once she started, there'd be nothing *quick* about it and she'd never make it to work on time.

"What are you doing tonight?" he mumbled at the sensitive spot under her ear.

"Hopefully doing you." She sounded breathless.

He chuckled. God, that low, sexy laugh vibrated through her body, awakening all her good parts.

"Want to go to dinner?"

Jade turned in his arms. "Dinner?"

"Yeah, you know…when you put food into your mouth around six PM. It's called dinner."

"I'm offering to give you all-access sex and you want dinner?"

"*All* access?" He raised an eyebrow.

"Well, there's one area that's a no-go zone, but everything else is wide open." She grinned.

"I love it when you talk dirty, Freckles."

He was teasing, but his words caused her stomach to do cartwheels. "And you should see the underwear I'm wearing."

"More superheroes?"

She slid a hand up his chest and hooked it behind his neck, drawing his mouth an inch from her lips. "You'll have to find out for yourself."

Puss in Boots. This time her undies were a cartoon character, and Nate couldn't be more turned on. It made him want to see her whole collection. What kind of sicko did that make him?

After ditching his dinner ideas they'd ordered pizza and came back to his house. Now they laid on the bed in a tangle of arms and legs. The sound of rough, heavy breathing was the only noise in the room. Damn, sex with Jade just kept getting better and better.

He pushed the mass of red hair from her face and peered down at Jade's expression. His chest puffed. Hell yeah, he put that satisfied look on her face.

Her pretty blue eyes blinked up at him. "I think I'm dead. As in I've died and gone to heaven. Even though what you did was definitely sinful and could only come from the devil himself."

There was no higher compliment. "You were pretty wicked yourself."

She stretched, placing her breasts dangerously close to

his mouth. "We make a good team. I could get used to this." Her eyes widened. "I mean for as long as you're in town. I'll totally forget all about you once you leave. No, no, that sounds so slutty. I'll remember you, but I won't be pining for you…" She buried her face in his chest. "I should stop talking now."

He tugged lightly on her hair, making her look at him again. "I'll remember you too."

Their eyes locked. But the sound of his mobile phone broke the connection. Reaching to take it off the bedside table, he read the caller ID. Mike. With the time zone differences, they kept missing each other's calls.

"Sorry, I need to take this."

He quickly put on his boxer shorts, gave one last, longing glance at Jade, then left the room.

"Hey, man," Nate said.

"Finally," Mike answered. "You're a hard man to catch."

Nate chuckled. "I can say the same thing about you."

"Are you sure you can't get back sooner? You staying in the land down under is not making things easy for the band." Although Mike said it in jest, Nate could hear an underlying tone of resentment.

"Sorry, mate, I've got things to do here."

"I thought you were taking time off to relax?"

"I'm helping a friend out." Mike would crack a rib from laughing if Nate told him he was teaching a bunch of primary school kids music.

"You like the new songs I sent?"

They were typical Harvey's Territory stuff. Mike did a

great job. But did Nate like them? No, because they didn't move him when he listened to them. He didn't feel the emotions in the lyrics.

"The songs are awesome." It wasn't a full-blown lie. They *were* awesome, just not what he yearned to play.

"I've been talking to *Temp Rock* magazine, and they want to do an interview with you about the next leg of the tour."

"Okay, when I'm back in New York we'll set it up."

Mike was silent for a beat. "Umm, they don't want to wait that long. I told them you'd do a Skype call."

Nate pinched the bridge of his nose. "When?"

More silence and then, "Now."

"Now? What the fuck, man? I'm not ready to do this shit now. And what if I wasn't available?"

"I took a chance. And I know you have your gear with you, it won't take you long to slap it all on. The interview will only take twenty minutes, tops."

"Why the hell can't you do it?" Nate asked.

"I am, but they want you too or it's not happening."

"Then it's not happening."

Dorito was meowing and rubbing his body against Nate's legs. He went into the kitchen, opened a can of cat food he'd picked up that morning, and dumped it out into the bowl he'd also bought. He needed to feed the animal on something, and the dishes he ate from were not for cats.

"Come on, man. I already told him we'd do it. If we back out now, we'll look like dicks, and he'll no doubt write that about us."

Nate didn't care what the journalist wrote about them, but his band mates did, and he couldn't let them down. Shit. Now he had to suit up and play Nathan Harvey.

"Fine. I'll call you when I'm ready." With that, Nate hung up.

He strode into the bedroom, intending to tell Jade he had work to do. He knew he'd seem like an arsehole asking her to leave, but he couldn't stand for her to see him dressed up as Nathan Harvey. It never brought out the best in him. She'd already witnessed it firsthand.

But she was fast asleep, curled up on her side with the sheet pulled up to her chin. He didn't have the heart to wake her. Hopefully, the interview would be quick and he could get back into bed with her and wake her in a more pleasurable kind of way.

It took him about fifteen minutes to get on the costume that he kept stored in the spare room. The colored contacts were always the hardest. No matter how many times he put the suckers in his eyes, they never went in the first time. And the wig scratched like a bitch. He pulled on jeans, an old, worn-out t-shirt, and a denim jacket to hide his tattoo-less arms. He didn't need his stage clothes for an interview.

Now ready, he sat at the small kitchen table and opened his laptop. He connected with Mike and his friend's smiling face filled the screen.

"I'm ready," Nate said.

"Great. I'll buzz Clay in and we're good to go." Mike did whatever he had to do on the computer to start the group conversation, then Clay's face was on the screen.

"Hi, boys. Nice to see you. Thank you so much for taking the time for this interview," Clay said a little too enthusiastically. Nate hated journos who tried to suck up his arse.

After a bit of small talk, he fired off the questions. The same questions Nate had heard thousands of times. What's your inspiration for the new album? What's your favorite city? Are you looking forward to the next leg of the tour? These he answered on autopilot. They didn't need much thought.

Then the sleazier questions started. The ones they think will make them sound cool for asking. What country has the hottest women? What band member sleeps around the most? Do you leave a woman in each city?

Nate was about to tell Clay to get fucked and it wasn't any of his business when the journalist's eyes lit up and he beamed. "Who's the lovely lady?"

Nate whipped his head around and found Jade standing at the entrance of the kitchen wearing his t-shirt. And from the light shining from the living room, her silhouette showed she wore nothing underneath. Not even her Puss in Boots undies.

"Oh God, I'm so sorry to interrupt," she gasped. A hand flew to her chest as she spun on her heels and disappeared.

"Got yourself a hot one there. I love a fiery redhead. They're wild in and out of the sack. Is she a natural?" Clay gave a sleazy smirk.

Anger percolated in Nate's gut. Not because Jade had

walked into the kitchen, but because of Clay's derogatory remarks. He made it sound like some cheap woman was occupying Nate's bed.

Just as Nate was about to tell Clay to stick the rest of the interview up his arse, Mike jumped in, thanking him for the interview and ending the call before Clay asked more questions or made any more salacious comments.

"Fuck!" Nate spat. "What are my chances of that getting cut from the interview?"

Mike shook his head. "I'm afraid low. Let me call our lawyer and see if she can do anything about stopping it. Who's the woman? Is she a hook-up while you're in town?"

Now he wanted to put his hands around Mike's throat. But isn't that what she was? What they agreed to? Having Mike say it that way degraded his time with her, and Jade was anything but cheap.

"She's a friend." That's all he needed to say.

"Okay. Well, hopefully your *friend* isn't splashed all over the internet tomorrow."

Nate fucking hoped so too. He hung up and went in search of Jade.

Chapter 16

When Nate, still dressed as his rock star persona, stormed into the bedroom Jade was putting on her shoes, trying to ignore her jittery stomach.

"I didn't mean to interrupt," she said.

He pulled off his wig, tossed it on a chair in the corner of the room, and ran his fingers through his flattened hair. "It's okay. You couldn't have known."

So why the cold stare when she walked in on him? "I should go." Thick tension curled around Nate. She wasn't staying where she wasn't wanted.

"Before you do, I need to tell you something."

Okay, wow. He wasn't even going to try to sway her to stay? But to show he hadn't upset her, she lightened the mood and said, "You're Batman?" Maybe he had multiple disguises she didn't know about.

He lifted an eyebrow. "I'm not Batman."

"That's a shame, I would've liked a ride in the Batmobile." Joking was better than facing his rejection.

The corners of his mouth twitched. "Sorry to disappoint." Then his mood darkened again. "You walked in on an interview with a music magazine. Those journos are like sharks, swimming around waiting to take a bite of anything juicy they can find. When he saw you, he knew he'd hit the jackpot. You were fresh bait, and he smelled blood."

Jade's stomach sank. By the somber tone in Nate's voice, this wouldn't end well. "What's Jaws going to do?"

"Most likely he'll put you in the article he's writing."

"Did you mention I can play the tambourine? Since it's a music mag he may want to know my musical abilities." When he didn't crack a smile, she knew it was serious.

"*Nathan Harvey* has never been photographed with a woman so intimately before. Never been involved in any kind of sordid scandal. This could blow up."

"How big?" Her legs shook, and she sat on the edge of the bed.

"We'll try to stop it. He only got a quick glimpse of you, so no one will know who you are."

Blowing out a sigh of relief, she smiled. "That doesn't sound so bad. I'm sure everything will be fine."

Everything was not fine.

At six o'clock in the morning she was woken up by the constant buzzing of messages hitting her mobile. But before she could look at any of them, Nate was calling.

When she answered, his voice boomed from the phone. "Jade, I'm so sorry it got out."

She pushed her tangled hair out of her face and sat up. "The article? That was quick."

"No, the photo. Clay, the fucking scum, sold it to the trashy tabloid *SRC Magazine*, and they've splashed it all over the internet."

Her brain still foggy with sleep, his words didn't make much sense. Last night they'd been talking about an article, not a photo. "What photo?"

He sighed. "When you were standing behind me, Clay took a screenshot, then he cropped out his and Mike's faces so it left only you and me."

Jade bolted upright, all fogginess evaporating. "I was only wearing your shirt!" *Oh God.*

"I'm sorry," Nate said again. "I'm hoping they won't figure out who you are. At the moment you're known as the *mystery redhead.*"

She had a sinking feeling, judging by the constant buzzing of messages from her phone, that her identity had gotten out. "I've got to go," she said and hung up.

Noise from the street had her bounding out of bed. She padded barefoot to the front window and peered outside. Camped on her lawn was a media circus. Men and women with microphones and cameras paced eagerly in front of her house, and two white vans were parked on the street. What the hell?

She swiped through her phone. Message after message from friends and family were almost identical. *You're involved with Nathan Harvey? OMG, I love him!* Ava and Lauren had messaged that they were on their way with coffee and chocolate muffins. Liz had sent a bunch of angry-faced emojis with *how could you keep this from me? I'm his number one fan!*

Nate must not have gotten the update on the solved mystery of the redhead.

Waiting for her friends to arrive, she sat at the kitchen table, not sure what to do next, when another text buzzed her phone. This one from Nate. *Fuck, they know. I'm on my way over.*

No. He couldn't be seen here. What if someone recognized him? It might expose the anonymity he'd worked hard to keep. It wasn't worth the risk. She called to stop him.

He answered on the first ring. "I'm nearly at your place. I don't know how they found out who you are."

"That doesn't matter right now. You can't come over here."

"Why the hell not? I put you in this mess, I need to fix it." She could hear the anger in his voice vibrating through the phone.

"You'll have to do that at your place because mine is crawling with cameras. Someone might recognize you."

"Shit," he spat then was silent for a beat. "It doesn't matter. You shouldn't have to deal with this alone."

"I'm not going to be alone. Lauren and Ava are coming over. And I have to tell them who you really are. I can't keep something like this a secret from them any longer. I promise they won't say anything."

"If you trust them, I do too. God, Jade, I never meant for this to happen."

"It's not your fault. Besides, I'm sure it will blow over soon enough. Surely Justin Bieber will do something stupid, and we'll be forgotten."

He laughed, and even the sound through the phone caused her skin to tingle with delight. "If you need me at all today, just call."

"I will. I'll see you this afternoon at class."

"You still want to do that? These people will follow you everywhere."

The thought of strangers tracking her every move gave her the creeps. "I don't want to let the kids down." A knocking sounded at her front door. "The girls are here. I'll talk to you later."

She hung up and ran to the door, opening it a crack to make sure it wasn't a reporter. When she saw her friends, she opened the door a little wider so she could hide behind it but enough for them to squeeze through. Once they hurried into the house, she quickly shut and locked the door.

Lauren held a bag of muffins, Ava had coffees, and they both had identical shocked expressions on their faces.

Ava was the first to break the silence. "Nathan fucking Harvey! What the hell? One minute you're eyeballing your music teacher, and the next you land the lead singer of one of the coolest rock bands!" She set the tray holding the takeaway cups on the coffee table and slammed her hands on her hips. "I don't think I know who you are anymore." Ava's lips trembled, and her eyes misted.

"Oh crap, I'm sorry, Ava. This is all a big misunderstanding. Please don't cry." Her friend, who she'd never seen cry in the whole time they'd known each other, now cried at the drop of a hat.

"These bloody hormones are making me crazy." She sniffed.

Lauren's bag of muffins joined the coffees. "What a coincidence both men are musicians. Have a thing for guitar players, do you?"

Jade dropped onto the couch. "It looks that way."

Her friends sat opposite Jade and waited for her to explain. Finally she'd be able to tell them the secret she'd been keeping, and relief lifted from her shoulders. "Nate Miller and Nathan Harvey are the same person."

Two blank faces stared back at her.

She waved a hand in front of them. "Hello. Did you hear what I said?"

They blinked a couple of times, then Lauren said, "But...but...how?"

"Nate *Miller* uses a disguise when he goes on stage, because he doesn't want the fame and everything that goes with it to intrude on having a normal life."

"I can understand that." Lauren nodded. Her husband, Jack Henderson, was a famous ex-football player, and even after retiring years ago from the sport, he still attracted media attention. It had taken her friend some time to get used to it. "Someone as big as Nathan Harvey would get people following him everywhere. But if he didn't want the attention, why go into the music industry?"

"His dad was also a famous musician with a huge following."

"Cold Revenge." Ava's eyes lit up. "I've heard of them."

"Yes, you're right. His dad died when he was young, and he wanted to keep his memory alive."

"That's so sweet," Lauren said.

"The guy you're truly, madly, crazily in lust with is Nathan Harvey. This is so freaking awesome. I can't wait to tell Nick," Ava announced.

"No!" Jade cried. "This can never get out. He's gone to a lot of trouble keeping this a secret. You can't even tell your husbands. Promise me."

After a bit of grumbling, mostly from Ava, they both agreed.

Lauren opened the bag of muffins, handed one to each of them, and passed them the coffees. "So how do *you* know this big secret?"

"Remember when I took Liz to a concert?" When they both nodded, she continued. "It was Nate's band, and Liz got us backstage."

"You never told us you went backstage." Ava glared. "I've always had a thing for the drummer. Is he even hotter in person?"

"I didn't get to meet him. Liz and I got separated, and

when I went looking for her, I got lost and found Nathan instead. He wasn't with the party. He got a little too close, my finger got tangled in his wig, and I accidentally pulled it off."

Again, her friends stared at her with frozen expressions. Ava broke the connection and reached for another muffin. "I need more chocolate to hear the rest of this story. This is freaking incredible."

"There's not much more to tell. He threatened to sue if I told anyone."

"What a jerk." Ava's tune changed as she took a mouthful of muffin.

"I thought so too. But he happened to be a friend of Toby's and volunteered his time to teach the kids music and donated a truck load of the best quality instruments I've ever seen."

"What a sweetheart," Lauren said, then sipped her coffee.

"That sure won me over," Jade had to admit.

"And now you're having sex with a hot rock star." Ava placed a hand on her heart. "I'm so proud. And then he'll take you on tour, and you'll be the envy of every woman in the world."

Jade leaned back on the couch and stared up at the ceiling. "When he leaves Brimland Point I'm not going with him. This is only temporary."

Her heart squeezed at the thought of him leaving. But she knew it would happen, and she would be okay, because they were only having fun. Nothing more.

Before her friends could drill her with more questions, she sat up. "I need to get ready for work, but I don't know how to get past those vultures."

Ava rubbed her belly and grinned. "Leave it to me."

Chapter 17

*J*ade didn't have to worry about the journalists pointing their cameras directly in her face when they left the house. When Ava had clutched her belly, screaming at the top of her lungs that she needed to get to the hospital because her water had broken, they parted like the Red Sea, letting them pass. Jade hoped when the real time came, Ava wasn't so vocal. But for now, it was perfect.

They bundled Ava in the backseat, Jade jumped in the passenger seat, and Lauren took the wheel. Tires squealing as they drove away from the house like they were being chased by the hounds from hell.

When they got to school, another media camp was positioned in front of the gates. "Drive into the teacher's parking lot, and I'll get out there," Jade instructed.

"Maybe you should take the day off," Lauren suggested as she pulled into a spot.

Jade shook her head. "I won't let them stop me from

doing my job. Thanks for the lift." She got out of the car and hurried into the building.

The first place she stopped was Toby's office. She needed to warn him about the reporters. He was on the phone when she entered the room.

"No, I'm not available now or anytime in the future to discuss my teacher." Toby rolled his eyes at Jade as she took a seat. Well, he'd already heard the news. "You can bribe me with whatever you like. Our school is well-equipped, we have everything we need. I'm not allowing you on school property, and if I see you, I'll be calling the police. Have a nice day." With that, he hung up, blew out a breath, and slumped in the chair.

"We could've used new computers," Jade joked.

Toby pinched the bridge of his nose. "That's the fifth call I've gotten this morning." His gaze lifted to the clock on the wall. "And it's not even eight-thirty."

"New computers, sports equipment, art supplies, sunshades for the playgrounds. We're good with musical instruments." She smirked.

"Jade, this isn't funny." Toby frowned.

No, it wasn't, but it was either joke about it or curl into a ball and wait until it passed. "I'm sorry."

"This is Nate's fault. He should have stayed away from you. Now I have to deal with journalists wanting information about my teacher."

Her eyebrows drew together. "This won't affect my job, will it?"

"No, but I'm sure there'll be parents complaining. I'll deal with them, but you'll need to keep a low profile."

She sighed with relief.

"No playground duty for a few days. The media may not be allowed to set foot in the school, but they can still photograph you from the street. And try not to get any more scantily dressed photos on the internet again."

"Scantily dressed…since when do you talk like an eighty-year-old man?"

He pointed at the door. "Get to work."

"I wish you'd drop this act and be yourself," Fi-Fi said as Nate sat at her kitchen table sipping coffee strong enough to tar a road.

Today his grandmother was dressed in neon pink tights and a loose-fitting yellow top. She was tucked under the kitchen sink trying to fix a leak.

"I *wish* you'd let me do that for you," he said, ignoring her remark.

She crawled out of the small space, rose, and wiped her hands on a rag. "Why? I'm capable of doing it myself." She turned on the tap, ducked her head, and peered under the sink. "Leak fixed. Now, explain how your pretty teacher, looking like she'd come straight out of your bed, wound up on the net with you dressed as Nathan Harvey? Obviously, she knows your secret, because there's no way you could use your disguise during sex without her noticing. Unless you do it doggy style, then maybe you could get away with it. But then there's foreplay, so it would be too tricky."

Nate groaned and covered his face with his hands. How many thirty-four-year-old men had these kinds of conversations with their grandmothers? Probably not many. He wanted to block his ears with his fingers and sing loudly enough that he couldn't hear Fi-Fi talk about sex.

"Can we change the subject please?" he asked.

"We're both adults here, and sex is a part of life. For a while I was getting worried you weren't having any at all. Thank goodness for Jade. Maybe she can drag you out of your bad mood."

Where was a sinkhole to fall into when he needed one? "I haven't been in a bad mood," he grumbled.

Fi-Fi lifted an eyebrow. "Yes, you have, and I know why."

Did he even want to ask? But he did anyway, because she'd only tell him whether or not he wanted to hear it. "Why?"

"Because of your disguise. Because it's stopping you from doing what you really want to do."

He rubbed his hands on his thighs. "I want to play music and sing. I *am* doing what I love."

"You want to sing your *own* songs." She pointed a finger at him.

"They are my songs. I write most of them."

"Yes, but they sound just like your father's. You want to sing songs *you* love. Play music that inspires you and makes you happy."

But he'd made a promise to his father to keep his music alive, and that's what he intended to do. He finished the last of his coffee and rose. "I am happy, and I'm glad you're looking out for me, but I have to teach a class." He kissed Fi-Fi's cheek. "Love you."

He left the kitchen, but before he made it outside, he heard her call out, "Get yourself more of that teacher. She's good for you."

Nate didn't find Jade outside of the hall greeting the parents like she did every afternoon, and he had a good idea why. There seemed to be every parent, grandparent, auntie, uncle, and whatever other kind of relative lined up with the kids. He was only teaching grades one and two; there shouldn't be that many people. He didn't need to be Einstein to know why they were all there.

Then he saw Toby storming toward the crowd. "If you do not have a child attending music lessons, you need to leave the school grounds immediately." He spoke in his firm, principal's voice.

Go, Toby.

A few people shuffled their feet but didn't move. "If I need to tell you again, I will call Brimland Point Police Department and they can escort you out." He held out a phone like he meant business. And by the look on his face, he was deadly serious.

The crowd made their way off the grounds. But there were still a few too many people hanging around.

"You ladies," Toby said, pointing to three girls. "I know you're too young to be parents, and you're too old to be students here. Unless you want me to call the police, you better leave. My finger's about to hit the *call* button."

The girls sprinted away.

Toby walked over to Nate, who was keeping a low profile in the shade of a nearby tree. "Because of you I've had to patrol the school today. Do you know how many kids have *forgotten their lunches* and the parents have dropped them in?" When Nate shook his head, he continued. "A fucking shitload. I have better things to do with my time. Fix this mess."

If only he could. "This will blow over in a couple of days, and it will be old news."

"You better hope so," Toby grumbled. He stormed away and ushered the kids inside the building. Instead of the parents leaving like they normally did and picking up their kids when class was over, they hovered around the door.

Ducking his head, Nate quickly went inside, carefully making sure no one recognized him.

He found Jade pacing at the back of the hall. He told the kids to select their instruments and make as much noise as possible. They cheered, and a catastrophic sound filled the room. Enough noise for him to talk with Jade and not be heard.

Nate placed his hands on Jade's shoulders and turned her toward him. "Are you okay?"

"Yes." She plastered on a fake smile and looked away.

He placed a finger under her chin, pulling her head back to look at him. "Freckles, have they bothered you at school?"

She blew out a quick breath. "Apart from stalkers trying to come onto the grounds, where our kids should feel safe, and some abusive emails from parents, they haven't bothered me much."

He dropped his head for a beat. "I'm so sorry this has happened."

"This isn't your fault. I'll handle it. It's fine."

It wasn't *fine*. He could see it clearly in her tense expression. But this wasn't the time or place to discuss it further. "After class we'll talk."

She shook her head. "I have to visit my mum. I've been avoiding her calls all day. We can talk later."

He let go of her shoulders, and she walked over to the kids, clapping her hands to get their attention. Once they quietened down, she stepped back and let him take over the class.

But before they got started, Lachlan raised his hand. "Is Miss Brennan going to marry the rock star? My mummy said it would be exciting if she did."

He glanced over at Jade, and his heart tripped. If only their circumstances were different, maybe they could've had a future together. "Miss Brennan will find a better man to marry than a rock star. Now, let's see if you remember what you learned from the last lesson."

Because Lauren and Ava had driven her to school, Nate gave Jade a ride to her mother's house. As they pulled into the driveway, she dropped her head in her hands. Both

Connor and Kaitlin's cars were parked in front of the garage.

"What's the matter?" Nate asked.

"I was hoping to give a brief explanation to Ma and have her pass it onto my siblings. But no, my brother and sister *had* to be around to hear it firsthand."

"I can come in with you if you'd like."

When she looked at him, she could tell he was serious. He'd face her family to help her out.

"No, that's okay. I can handle them." With a sledgehammer if she needed to.

"I'll wait here for you so I can give you a ride home when you're done," he offered.

She shook her head. "My house isn't far. I can walk."

"Are you sure? I don't mind waiting."

"I could do with some fresh air to clear my mind. Trust me, I'll need it after talking to Connor."

Nate frowned. "Maybe I should come inside. He wasn't easy on you the other night."

"He's all bark. I can take him on."

Nate chuckled. "And you're all bite. I've got a few marks on my body to prove it."

Flaming hot heat rushed to her cheeks, and his chuckle turned into a laugh.

"I'm not complaining though," he assured her.

She nudged him with her elbow and got out of the car. He didn't leave until she was inside.

She found her mother, Connor, and Kaitlin gathered in the living room. They turned their attention toward her as she entered the room.

Kaitlin held a bowl of popcorn on her lap, shoveling handfuls in her mouth like she was getting ready to watch a movie. And Connor wore a scowl so hard it surprised her his face didn't crack.

Standing by the window, he crossed his arms over his chest. "Glad to see you're wearing a decent amount of clothes today. If you're not stripping off on a public beach, you're plastered all over the internet wearing practically nothing."

Jade rolled her eyes and sat next to Kaitlin and grabbed a handful of popcorn. "You're being so dramatic," she said before she shoved it in her mouth.

Connor pushed his fingers through his dark auburn hair, the waves so cooperative, they fell back into place. Why did she have to get the carrot-top and wild, untameable locks? Even Kaitlin's hair fell neatly to her shoulders.

"You think *I'm* being dramatic! Have you seen your bare arse online?" he said.

She inhaled sharply, and a piece of popcorn lodged in her throat. She coughed, and Kaitlin slapped her hard on her back to help dislodge it. Jade held out her hand for her to stop; she liked her lungs where they were.

When Jade got her breathing under control, she frowned at Connor. "Firstly, my arse was not bare. The photo was front-on, with all my bits covered. And secondly, this isn't my fault, so stop glaring at me like I did this on purpose."

"Wake up, Jade. He's a freaking famous musician who must have paparazzi following him everywhere. God, you were skinny-dipping with one guy the other night and half-naked with another the next. What the hell is wrong with you?"

Jade had enough of her brother yelling at her like a naughty child. Who was he to judge? Before becoming a police officer, he used to get up to some crazy shit too. Now the uniform he wore was like a stick up his arse.

"Wish I had a sex life like that," Kaitlin mumbled into her popcorn.

"Not that it's any of your business, but it's not what it looks like. And will you sit down? My neck is getting sore looking up at you."

He dropped onto the couch in front of her. It surprised Jade that he did what she'd asked.

"How the hell is this not what it looks like?" The belligerent tone was still the same.

Jade blew out a frustrated breath. "I wasn't with two different men. Not that it's anyone's business if I was." She glanced briefly at her mother who was sitting quietly through the conversation. Yes, she was an adult who could do as she pleased, but it didn't make it any easier talking about her sex life in front of her mother.

"Oh, really? Because the two guys I've seen you with look nothing alike."

"I'm glad. It works," she said.

Connor shook his head. "What the hell does that mean? What works?"

"Nate's disguise. Nate Miller is the guy you met the other night. Nathan Harvey is the musician. They are the same person."

Her family sat still and silent. Then Connor and Kaitlin shot questions like bullets at her.

She held up her hand. "Whoa. I can only answer one question at a time. And none of yours, Kait, you perve. God, can't you see Ma's in the room?"

The next hour Jade filled her family in on who Nate was and why he used a disguise. Once Connor learned she wasn't planning on doing most of the men in Brimland Point, he calmed down a touch. Kaitlin was beaming from ear to ear. She was hoping to get VIP tickets to their next concert.

From the moment Jade had walked into the house, her mother had remained silent, just watched and listened. Now her scrutiny was making Jade squirm in her seat.

Finally, not able to take the silence from her any longer, she said, "Just say it, Ma. You're ashamed of me, aren't you? Your good, Catholic girl is an embarrassment."

"That's not what I was thinking at all," her mother replied. "Yes, having my daughter half-naked on the internet wasn't what I wanted to see. But it's not your fault."

When Connor started to object, their mother threw him a sharp look, and he kept quiet. Jade wished she had that kind of control over him.

"No one's privacy should be invaded like that no matter who you are," her mother continued. "It's the dirty paparazzi who should be ashamed of themselves. Not my daughter."

"Go, Ma!" Kaitlin cheered.

"But I don't want this Nate leading you astray. You've had an upbringing with strong morals. I'd hate for you to throw all that away. I'm hoping there is more of a connection between the two of you than just…just…"

"Are you trying to say sex, Ma?" Kaitlin giggled.

Connor scrubbed a hand over his face.

Their mother blushed rosy red.

Jade's cheeks burned.

"Just be careful," her mother said.

"I will. I'd like to say it was great spending time with you this afternoon but…" She shrugged. "I'm outta here."

"Where are you going?" Connor demanded.

Jade rose from the couch and slapped her hands on her hips. "Seriously, bro, you are so uptight. When was the last time you got any action? Do you need to go to that house in town with the red light outside? Maybe someone can loosen you up a little."

Their mother sighed. "Why must you have these conversations when I'm around?"

"Because every time I do something, we seem to need a freaking family meeting." Jade left with Connor scowling, her mother shaking her head, and Kaitlin grinning like a lunatic.

Chapter 18

a balmy breeze tussled Jade's hair as she walked to her house. As she rounded the corner of her street, a group of journalists stood on her lawn. She quickly turned to go back the way she'd came, but they spotted her before she could take two steps. A ring of people with microphones and cameras hurried over to her, pointing them at her face. The bright light blinded her, and she held up her hand to shield her eyes.

"Jade, tell us how you met Nathan Harvey."

"How long have you been seeing each other?"

"He's never gone public with a relationship before. Does this mean you two are serious?"

"How does it feel to be the envy of thousands of women around the world?"

One after another they fired questions at her. She spun around in circles, searching for a gap to squeeze through to make a bolt for her house, but they closed in tight, giving her no room to breathe.

"Get the fuck away from her," said a menacing voice, one she recognized well, and she wanted to sag with relief.

Keeping his head low, and wearing a black cap and dark sunglasses even though the sun had just sunk behind the mountains, Nate elbowed and barged his way through the wall of people, grabbed her by the hand, and pushed his way out of the crowd. Once free from the cage, they made a run for Nate's car parked on an angle on the road like he'd just stopped it in the middle of the street in his rush to get to her. The group followed close behind as they dived into the car. Nate had left it running, and they burned out of there before anyone reached them.

"Those people are fucking arseholes." Nate slammed his hand against the steering wheel. "Are you okay?"

"Yes-s." Her teeth chattered and her body shook as if she were cold when outside was a warm, summer evening.

He shot a quick glance in her direction. "Shit." He pulled over into a small parking area on the side of the road. "You're shaking and as white as a sheet."

"Unfortunately, that's j-just my n-natural complexion." She tried to smile but her lips wobbled.

He threw off his hat and glasses, pulled her as close as he could with the car's console between them, and rubbed her arms, trying to warm her up. "I think it's a little more than that. You're so white even your freckles have disappeared."

"I told you I've spent a lot of money trying to hide those things. Who knew all I needed was a run-in with the media to get the job done?" The shaking eased, and her body was warming up. It felt so good being wrapped in his arms. "Won't they wonder who came to my rescue?"

"I'll have someone leak it was your overprotective brother. That's easy enough to believe." He tried to smile but failed. "I'm sorry this is happening to you."

"It's not your fault. Why were you at my house?" she asked.

"I knew they'd still be hanging around and that you would walk into…well, exactly what you did. I wanted to pick you up before you got home, but I was too late. I arrived just as they surrounded you." His harsh tone belied the gentle stroking along her arm.

She sighed with pleasure, the tension slowly easing from her body. "You said it will blow over soon. Do you really think that will happen?"

"Yeah, I do. But the next couple of days will be a lot like what you've experienced today." The dashboard lights illuminated the frown on his face.

"Maybe I'm the one who needs to wear a disguise now. I've always wanted to be blonde. I hear they have more fun." She laughed, trying to lighten the mood.

He twisted a curl around his finger and gently tugged so her face drew closer, their lips almost touching. "I love your hair. There's no chance in hell you're covering it up. It's fucking sexy when it's wild and crazy. Makes me imagine all the ways I can mess it up." His eyes flashed heat.

The tremble of her heart vibrated behind her ribs. He loved her hair. No man had ever said that before. If Nate kept saving her from creeps and sweet-talking her like that, she could easily fall for him. But she couldn't let that happen, so she did the next best thing—kissed him.

The slow-burning kiss shot fierce desire through her veins, but it wasn't enough, her body needed more contact. Breaking off the kiss, she lifted herself over the console and straddled Nate's lap, wiggling to get comfortable.

He hissed at the sensation then cupped her face and brought her lips back to his mouth. Skimming his hands down her body, he gripped her butt, guiding her to rock against what was growing hard and strong underneath her. She didn't need encouragement. It was exactly what she wanted to do too.

Nate's hand wove its way behind her head, and he buried his fingers into her hair. "So sexy," he said as his lips skimmed her mouth, along her jaw, and down to her neck.

Sucking in a deep breath, Jade tilted her head to the side, and his tongue swirled in circles against her pounding pulse.

God, Nate made her body tremble like she'd never experienced before. The few men she'd been with had never set her on fire with a mere kiss. She'd never lost herself in the passion of the moment. It was like all those times she was only going through the motions.

Sure, she'd had fun, but this…this was another level. It was out of this world. And she couldn't get enough of him.

"Have you ever made out in a car before?" she asked, tugging at his shirt, jerking it over his head and throwing it toward the backseat.

She ran her hands along his smooth, firm chest. Muscles bunched under her fingertips, and his eyes hooded right before he leaned forward and placed his mouth on her breast, ripping a moan from her lips.

"That's another teenage fantasy I never experienced," he mumbled against her chest.

She sighed and broke out in goose bumps as his warm breath tickled her skin. "Man, you've missed out. It's a good thing you met me to show you the way."

Nate chuckled low and deep. "Thank God for that."

A loud knock pounded at the foggy window, and they sprung apart.

"Out of the car please," came a stern, firm voice.

"Oh God!" Jade scrambled off Nate's lap, kneeing him in the groin in her haste to get to the passenger seat.

"Fuck," he hissed, cupping himself.

"Sorry," she said as she leaned over into the backseat to look for Nate's shirt.

Another knock sounded at the window. "Out of the car now."

The familiar voice was not happy. God, did Connor have a freaking tracking device connected to her she didn't know about? Jade fumed as she busily searched for the shirt.

Nate must have opened the window because Jade felt a cool breeze on the back of her legs. Then someone groaned. "Not you again. And that arse up in the air better not be my sister!" He yelled so loud she was sure the entire city could hear.

Jade wiggled back into her seat, leaned over Nate, who was still shirtless—if she had her way, it would be twenty-four hours a day—and glared at her brother through the open window. "Are you *following* me?"

"No. I was on my way to work and drove past a fogged-up car practically rocking off its springs. Do you realize this is a residential area? There are houses all around you. And you." He pointed a finger, and luckily not a gun, at Nate. "Haven't you gotten my sister in enough trouble? Get a fucking room, or I swear to God, if this shit keeps happening, I'm arresting both your arses. I don't care who the fuck you are." With that, he stormed away.

Jade and Nate sat in stunned silence for a beat then burst out laughing. "Oh my God. Can my life get any crazier?" She giggled into her hands.

"For a second I thought I'd get shot." Nate chuckled.

"He came close," she joked. Well, she hoped she was joking.

"We should go, in case he comes back and really arrests us." He flicked a glance toward the backseat. "Any luck finding my shirt?"

"Nope. You don't need it anyway."

His eyebrow rose. "I don't?"

"Why would anyone want to cover up a body like that?" Her hand slid over his chest and tattoo. She would never get sick of the sight or feel of him.

As her hand wandered a little south, he clamped it in his own. A flare of heat shot from his eyes. "I have a better place to finish this than in my car."

She pointed to the street. "What are you waiting for?"

Chapter 19

*T*he next day after school, Jade still couldn't get inside her house without a police escort—Connor. Sometimes her brother came in handy even though he was the biggest pain in the arse.

Nate had tried to convince her to go home with him, but she needed to work from home and write reports for her students. As tempting as his offer was—his whispered, wicked promises caused her knees to weaken—she was too far behind to keep putting her work off.

What would the media do if they found out she'd spent last night with Nathan Harvey? They'd go nuts, that's what.

As she made her way into the bedroom, the package her father sent sat unopened on the chest of drawers. He'd called a few times the past week, and she let it go to voicemail, then texted an excuse about being in a meeting and she'd call back.

She picked up the parcel, sat on the edge of the bed,

and opened it. A long, navy-blue box was inside. She lifted the lid. Nestled in the velvet lining, she found an emerald stone attached to a silver, intricate chain. She fingered the cool gem; it was beautiful. Next, she read the card.

To my birthday girl.

When I saw the colors of this stone, it reminded me of you. Beautiful and bright.

I hope you had a wonderful birthday.

Miss you, sweetheart, and I hope to see you soon.

Love, Dad xx

All her life, her father had missed important events. Birthdays, dance recitals, and her university graduation just to name a few. His job as an airline pilot had him traveling around the world and hardly ever home. At first, he'd only flown around Australia, and he'd be gone a couple of days at a time. But when he flew internationally, the time away stretched longer and longer, until one day, he never came home.

Over the years, he called her regularly, but depending on the time zone of the country he was in and their work schedules, they often missed each other.

Even after all this time, it still hurt that he left his family. His little girl. The daughter who followed him around like a shadow. The one who wanted to grow up and be a pilot like her dad. But when he didn't come home, and chose his work over family, she decided she never wanted a job that would take her away from loved ones. A part deep in her heart believed maybe he didn't love them enough to want to stay. And that's what cut the most.

She couldn't put off calling him back any longer and pulled her phone from her pocket.

After three rings, he answered. "Hi, shortcake."

He'd given her the nickname Strawberry Shortcake because of the color of her hair. The name got shortened over time.

"Hi, Dad. I hope I haven't caught you at a bad time?" She could hear rustling through the phone.

"No, just heading out to the airport."

"I won't keep you. I just wanted to say thanks for the gift. It's beautiful."

"I'm glad you like it. Sorry I didn't get it to you on time. You know how it is when I'm halfway around the world."

Yeah, she knew what it was like. It meant she rarely had her father in her life.

"I'll be flying into Sydney next month, and I have time off, so I'll be heading down to Brimland Point. I'd loved to get you kids together to hang out for a few days. I miss you guys so much." More noises in the background and someone calling his name.

"Sounds great," she said with exaggerated enthusiasm. The words clogged her throat. "I can hear you're busy, so I'll talk to you later. Have a safe flight."

"Okay, shortcake. Love you."

"Love you too."

When the call ended, she blew out a long, shuddery breath and flopped on her back on the bed. She always looked forward to seeing him, and they had fun while together, but every time he left, it still chipped away at her heart. She'd learned to mask the pain. As a kid, she'd cry and cling to him, trying to stop him from walking out the door. But as an adult, she smiled and waved him off. She'd never let him see the pain that twisted in her heart.

One good thing about their conversation—he never mentioned her affair with Nathan Harvey that was splashed over the internet. Being in the sky so much didn't allow a lot of time to catch up on the latest news. And by the quick call, catch up on how his family was doing.

Nate finished the last song of his set. The three new tracks he'd written over the past few days had gotten a great reaction from the crowd at Jovi's.

His muse for the lyrics was one sexy as hell redhead who wove into his every thought. He couldn't get her out of his head and thought it would be cathartic to pour it all on paper. They were the best songs he'd ever written. It was like a damn had burst open, and all these new ideas poured out.

Already he'd sold two songs to an up-and-coming singer Roan Blake who was getting a lot of attention from record companies, and Nate was sure he'd soon see the songs flying up the charts.

Finding Toby sitting in a booth, he slid him a Heineken he'd grabbed at the bar and sat down.

"You played good stuff tonight." Toby pushed his glasses up the bridge of his nose then clinked his bottle against Nate's. "Looks like you're building a following." His gaze scanned the packed pub.

"Thanks." Nate took a sip of his beer.

Toby smirked, "Although, the new tunes are too girly for me. Since when did you turn soft and start singing love songs?"

Nate flipped him the bird.

Toby laughed.

"Just trying something different," Nate explained.

"Can't imagine your band mates playing that stuff."

"It's not for the band. Mike's got new stuff written that we've been working on. Sounds good too." If he said it out loud often enough, maybe he'd believe it. Not that they were crap songs; they were actually the best Mike had written—and mostly without his input.

But the more Nate wrote and played his own stuff, the more the band's songs didn't appeal. Once he got back on the road and sang with Harvey's Territory again, he'd enjoy the music more. He was keeping his fingers crossed and hoped it to be true.

"Not long now and you'll be leaving to go on tour again."

A sinking feeling weighed heavy in Nate's gut, but he pushed it aside. The time to leave was approaching sooner than he liked. And Mike was bugging him to come home early because he wanted to record the new songs for the re-released album that would coincide with the next leg of the tour.

"You don't look too excited about it," Toby said.

How he felt must have showed on his face. "Enjoying my time off, that's all," he said as he picked at the corners of the label on the beer bottle.

"And enjoying your time with Jade too?" Toby raised a questioning eyebrow. When Nate didn't comment, Toby added, "Now she's the one in hiding from the media while you get to live a carefree life. I hope this dies down for her soon."

Yeah, he did too. "I hate how I've put Jade in this position. The vultures keep circling her because they want to know where I am. I have an idea that might take the attention from her."

"Oh yeah, what?" Toby asked.

"I'll let you know when I've figured out the details." He pushed his barely-touched beer away and rose from the booth. "I've got one more set. I'll see you later."

With that, he walked back on stage, and the crowd cheered at his arrival. He sat on the stool, propped the guitar on his thigh, and played a song that spoke of love, the kind that lasts forever.

Chapter 20

"Seriously? I can't even buy coffee without you people following me?" Jade snatched the packet of beans off the shelf, stomped over to the check-out, and slammed it on the counter.

If she didn't need her coffee fix so badly, she would never have attempted to dodge the media on her lawn to run to the grocery store. And in her haste to get to her car, she'd forgotten to take her Homer Simpson slippers off. And of course, the paparazzi were quick to take that shot, and a couple of them even followed her.

"I don't suppose you can call security and get these jerks kicked out of here, can you?" she said to the young cashier who stared wide-eyed at her and then at the two men standing behind her.

"All we want is to ask you a few questions and we'll leave you alone," one pap said before the girl could answer.

Jade paid and rushed out of the store. Tweedledum and Tweedledee followed.

"Ms Brennan!" they called, running fast for two short, stumpy people and reaching her car before she did. "A couple of questions please." They panted.

She blew out a frustrated breath. "If I answer, will you promise to go away and leave me alone?"

They nodded in unison. That would take care of two of them, but what about the five others outside her house? Maybe when they realized they'd lost their chance at an exclusive, she'd be old news and they'd pack up and move on.

Mind made up, she said, "You've got one minute, and then I'm gone."

Both of their eyes lit up with excitement, like they'd won the lottery. Tweedledum asked the questions while Tweedledee pulled out his phone, she assumed to take video. Damn, she should have worn something cuter than the conservative work shirt and skirt.

"Where did you meet Nathan Harvey?"

"At one of his concerts," she answered.

Tweedledum's shoulders sagged, and he gave his accomplice a disappointed look. "Oh, so you're just a groupie he picked up at a show?"

Tweedledee went to put his phone back into his pocket.

"God no," she exhaled on a huff of breath. Why did everyone think she was a groupie? Then she noticed the excited expressions were back and the phone pointed back at her face. She bit her tongue. Oh crap, she'd put her foot in it.

"You're not a groupie? This *is* a relationship? How long have you been together and hiding it?"

"Oh, look at the time." She flicked out her wrist even though she wasn't wearing a watch. "That's more than a couple of questions, and your minute is up." She tried pushing past them, but they blocked the access to her car door.

"Come on, Ms. Brennan, give us a little more," Tweedledum begged.

Jade slapped her hands on her hips. "Can you please get out of my way?"

He ignored her request. "Why do you and Nathan keep such a secret relationship?"

When they still wouldn't budge, she moved to the passenger side of the car, unlocked the door, and got in before they could stop her. Then she ungracefully climbed over the console and dropped into the driver's seat. Turning on the ignition, she pulled out of the carpark and flipped the paparazzi the bird.

———

Toby hung up the phone when Jade walked into his office. Every time she came to see him lately, he wore a scowl at whoever he was talking to. Nine out of ten times it had something to do with her. And by the way he frowned and scrutinized her, she knew she was the problem again.

Slumping into a chair, she waited for him to hit her with the latest. He blew out a long breath, yanked the glasses off his face, and threw them on the desk. This didn't look good.

"I see you've been busy again," he said, placing his elbows on the table.

Somehow, she didn't think he meant busy teaching students and organizing excursions. "What's happened now?" But she knew it must be about this morning's carpark interview.

Instead of explaining, he turned his laptop toward her. She leaned forward to get a better look at the screen and gasped. "Is that my arse?"

That was her car, and her undies with bright pink *bite me* written across her cheeks. The paparazzi, the big perverts, must have taken a photo as she scrambled into the driver's seat. She had no clue her skirt had lifted up in the struggle.

Another picture showed her flipping them off as she drove away. There was also a very unflattering photo of Jade buying coffee in her Homer Simpson slippers, mouth wide open as she spoke to the cashier.

The article's heading wasn't so great either.

Nathan Harvey's girlfriend, Jade Brennan, looks badly hungover and in need of sleep as she clings onto coffee beans.

The article was even worse.

. . .

The girlfriend of front man Nathan Harvey of Harvey's Territory looked a little worse for wear when she was spotted buying coffee at her local grocery store in Brimland Point. Wearing a wrinkled shirt, skirt, and cartoon character slippers, she looked far from a glamorous rock star's girlfriend.

When asked if Ms. Brennan's relationship with Mr. Harvey was only a fling, she replied, "God no", confirming that the two are in an exclusive and serious relationship.

After answering questions, she displayed odd behavior, jumping into the passenger side of her car to get to the driver's seat before driving away. A source close to Ms. Brennan confirmed she'd been out drinking until the early hours of the morning, which explained her disheveled appearance.

Close friends of Mr. Harvey are scratching their heads over this relationship and wondering how long it will take before his hectic touring lifestyle gets in the way.

Could this simple primary school teacher be the one to bag herself a rock star? Only time will tell.

Jade propelled from the chair like she'd been shot out of a cannon. "That's a lie! My clothes were not wrinkled."

Toby pinched the bridge of his nose. "*That's* what you got from reading the article?"

"Well, of course not." She blew out a long breath and dropped back into her chair. "The whole thing is bullshit." She rubbed her hands along her thighs. "How much trouble am I in now?"

She could see incoming calls lighting up Toby's phone, which he kept ignoring. She'd bet it wasn't an influx of student enrollments. Parents would be furious at seeing their teacher's butt splashed over the internet.

"Parents are complaining. They're questioning the morals of their teacher."

"And what did you say to them?"

"I told them they can't believe everything they read and that your work at this school is of high standard, and unless it affects class in any way, you will continue to teach."

Jade's shoulders slumped, and she blew out a relieved breath. "Thanks, Toby. I'm so sorry I've put you in this position. What can I do to make it up to you?"

"Stop getting your arse on the internet," he said as he shook his head.

"It's not like I planned it," she grumbled.

Toby's face grew serious. "I can't keep saving you. If anything else happens, whether or not it's your fault, I have to act on the parents' concerns."

"I promise I'll stay out of trouble." She made a cross sign over her heart.

Only seven students from grades four and five showed up to their music lesson. Jade wanted to cancel, it was hardly worth Nate's time, but he insisted he wanted to continue.

They hadn't had time to talk about the latest internet scandal, and she didn't know how he felt about what they had *quoted* her saying. Would he think she believed their time together was turning into something more? The lesson seemed to drag on forever. All she wanted to do was explain to Nate they'd made it all up and her feelings hadn't changed. Doubt made a sharp twist in her heart. No. Nothing had or would change.

Finally, class was over and she said goodbye to the kids and the parents picking them up. Nate was quiet as he packed away the instruments and placed the sheet music in folders. Her stomach tightened. Was he mad at her?

"I'm guessing you saw what happened this morning?" she said. Her stomach fluttered with nerves.

He nodded.

Crap, he is mad. "I'm so sorry. They followed me to the grocery store, and they told me they'd leave me alone if I answered a couple of questions. But they took what I said out of context and turned it into a lie. I'm such an idiot. I should never have agreed." The explanation flew from her mouth.

He threw a folder on the floor and sheet music scattered everywhere. "You are not an idiot." He stormed closer and dropped his hands on her shoulders. "Those fuckers had no right following you around."

"I didn't confirm we were in a relationship. He asked me something completely different."

Sliding his hands up and down her arms as if to soothe her, he said, "They know how to twist words around and make up bullshit."

"Are you mad at me?"

Nate's eyes grew wide. "Why the hell would I be mad

at you? I'm the one who put you in this position. You should be pissed at me. I'm sorry to have done this to *you.*"

She dropped her forehead on his chest for a beat, taking a moment to drag in a steadying breath. Emotions which felt deeper than friendship stirred in her chest, but she pushed them away before she looked back at him. "I'm starting to understand why you use a disguise."

"Makes life easier," he said.

"Until I screwed it all up."

"You screwed nothing up. This will pass. I hate how you're taking the brunt of it."

He cupped her face in his hands, and her gaze landed on his lips right before he covered her mouth with his. She melted against him, wrapping her arms around his waist for support.

"Lachlan forgot his school bag—"

They sprang apart and twirled around at the interruption. Lachlan's mother stood in the doorway gaping at them.

"Mrs. McKenna… We were… I'm…" Jade's shoulders slumped. There was nothing to say to explain what she walked in on. The look of disgusted horror on the woman's face said it all. Jade was in even bigger shit.

"You are not a fit role model for the children of this school. Mr. Lewis will hear from me," she spat as she picked up her son's bag and stormed out of the hall.

Toby had been hearing from a lot of parents lately. And this time, she knew he couldn't save her again.

Nate and Jade finished packing up the equipment then went in search of Toby, who they found pacing in his office. They both took a seat like they'd been called in for detention.

"Why the hell do you keep getting yourself in these situations?" He threw the question at Jade, but he didn't wait for a reply. "I had a furious parent in my office claiming you were having *sexual relations* in the school hall."

"Oh please," Jade scoffed. "It was a kiss."

"Yes, I know. When I eventually calmed her down, she agreed it was a kiss. But a very amorous one, inappropriate on school grounds. And she was also concerned with the amount of *men* you are seeing at the same time."

Devastation creeped along Jade's face. Nate clenched his hands into fists. He'd dumped this on her. Now her reputation was damaged because of him.

"Jade, I'm sorry, but until this dies down, I'll have to ask you not to come back to school." Toby grimaced like it pained him to say the words.

"You're firing me?" Jade squeaked.

Toby slumped onto his chair, placed his elbows on the desk, and dropped his head in his hands. "No, giving you annual leave. I'm hoping this will blow over soon and you can come back to work."

"And if it doesn't?"

Not meeting her gaze, he said, "We'll look into transferring you to a different school."

Nate couldn't listen to this anymore. "This is bullshit. This has nothing to do with Jade. They can't treat her this way. She's a great teacher, and her personal life shouldn't get in the way of that."

"Unfortunately, parents want squeaky clean teachers for their children. And as unrealistic as it sounds, I want that from my staff too."

"You're damn right it's unrealistic. Your teachers aren't robots. They have lives."

"You don't think I know that? But it should never bleed into their jobs, especially something negative. I tried calming the parents down as much as possible after the photos hit the internet. Most of them are understanding, but it's those few who kick up a stink until something is done about it. And after the kiss in the hall, I need to take action."

Jade nodded. "I understand."

Dammit, she shouldn't just accept this. "No. This isn't right. I'm the reason Jade's in this mess."

Toby threw up his hands. "You've got a disguise to hide behind. Unfortunately, Jade has to shoulder the blame."

He'd been playing with this thought since he'd spoken to Toby at Jovi's Pub. "What if I don't have it anymore?"

Toby and Jade both looked at him with confusion.

"Don't have what anymore?" she asked.

"My disguise."

Chapter 21

*J*ade sat in silence in Nate's car, trying to process the bomb he'd dropped in Toby's office. She hadn't complained when he drove her to his house instead of her own. He'd mumbled something about more reporters waiting there after the *relationship announcement*.

Surely he didn't really mean he'd give up his disguise.

When they walked into the house, Dorito greeted them. Jade picked him up and nuzzled his neck. "You're getting better-looking each day. Your fur is so soft and shiny."

"That's because I gave him a bath," Nate said as he sat on the living room couch.

Jade laughed. "A bath? Cats hate baths." She sat next to him. Dorito moved from one to the other to get some love.

"Not this cat. He lies in the water like he's floating in

the ocean in Hawaii. He's such a weirdo." To Jade's surprise, Nate patted Dorito affectionately.

"I think he likes it here," Jade said.

Nate gave Dorito another pat then put him on the floor. "He better not get too used to it, because I need to find him a new home soon."

The cat stretched and made his way to the corner of the living room and fell asleep on a bed Nate must have bought for him.

"I'll take him," she said.

"You don't have to."

"I want to." She'd have something to remember Nate. Even if it was a weirdo cat.

"That would be great."

After Jade could no longer use the distraction of Dorito to avoid what happened in Toby's office, she said, "You can't get rid of your disguise."

"Why not? I've caused you so much trouble. Christ, it's even cost you your job." He ran jerky fingers through his hair.

"I could do with some time off. Those kids can be draining." She tried to joke, but judging by his stern expression, it fell flat. She grabbed his hand. "It won't come to that. I'll have some time off, this will blow over, and I'll be able to go back to work and all will be forgotten." At least she hoped so.

He shook his head. "You're the one copping it all when this is my fault. If I let the world know about my disguise, no one will bother you again. *I'll* be hot news for the next few days and the attention taken off you."

"You've worked too hard to throw away your disguise. Think of why you did it in the first place. The anonymity allows you to have a normal life off the stage. Can you really deal with people following you around twenty-four-seven? Trust me, I've had a small taste and its crappy. I don't know how celebrities do it on a daily basis. No wonder they turn to drugs and alcohol." She gasped and covered her mouth. "Oh God, I'm so sorry, I didn't mean to sound so insensitive. I wasn't talking about your parents."

He tugged her arm to bring her closer, then lifted her so he could cradle her on his lap. "My parents thrived on the attention. The drugs and alcohol were a perk for them. It flowed freely at their parties until it eventually killed them. It's a big part of that world. One I never wanted to be involved in."

Wrapping her arm around his shoulders, she said, "And that's why you need to keep your disguise so you don't fall into the same trap."

He chuckled. "I'm old enough to know not to get messed up like that. If it was ten or more years ago, who knows? It could've been me shaving my head and beating a car with an umbrella."

"Oh, you think you'd go full Britney, do you?" She smirked.

He chuckled. "Hmm, maybe not."

Running her fingers through his dark sandy hair, she gently tugged it. "Good. It would be a shame to cut this off." And then with more seriousness, she added, "And it would be a shame for you to throw away everything you've worked hard for. What if the truth coming out put the band in jeopardy?"

He frowned. "What do you mean?"

"Your fans believe you're this tough, tattooed, hard rocker. If they find out you're clean-cut and as gentle as a pussycat—"

"I'm hardly a pussycat." He growled as he squeezed her tight.

She laughed. "You know what I mean. The real man is not the rock genius they know and love. You're still a fabulous musician—I'd buy your album." She grinned, and he laughed. "But you'll be different. Would Harvey's Territory fans be as accepting? Do you want to risk it?"

He stayed quiet for a moment, playing with a lock of her hair. She could see him weighing the decision in his mind. The struggle as to what to do was etched on his face.

"I'll be okay," she assured him. "The media will move onto something bigger and better in a few days. Surely there'll be a Kardashian flashing her arse in another magazine soon." She placed a feather-light kiss on his lips. "Keep the disguise."

He nodded and drew her in for a deeper kiss. Then he dipped his head, pressing his mouth to her throat, and mumbled, "You smell so good." His tongue licked her skin. "Taste even better."

Her heart hammered in her chest. What was it about this man that made her body turn to putty in his hands, or in this case, lips? Whatever it was she wished she could bottle it and pull it out to enjoy when he left. No, she wouldn't think about that. She was here with him now, enjoying the moment.

His hands swept down her arms and to the front of her shirt. He was quick to release the buttons, and in record time, her top was open and her chest exposed. Pushing the fabric from her shoulders, he cupped her breasts in his strong hands. His fingers stroked her raised nipples, and she shivered. His tongue replaced his hands, and the sensation nearly made her leap off his lap. This was torture of the best kind.

Straddling him, she dragged off his shirt, unbuttoned the fly of his jeans, and reached inside the soft denim only for his hand to clamp around her wrist.

"Why are you stopping me?" She gasped her displeasure.

"Because I want to take my time. You reach in there and it will be hard and fast."

"I like hard and fast. I'll take it." She made to reach in his jeans and was stopped a second time. She released a frustrated groan.

"I want to take my time," he said as he kissed her shoulder, neck, and the top of her breasts. "I want to taste every inch of you then start all over again."

Her stomach quivered. No, no, no. She could not go slow. Her heart couldn't take the emotion.

For the third time she reached in his pants, and again he stopped her. "Why are you doing this to me?" She tipped her head back and blinked up at the ceiling.

He laughed, and she gritted her teeth.

"Look, if you need to go slow because you have erectile dysfunction or something and are embarrassed to admit it, we can try this another time." She started to get off his lap, but he held her hips securely, moving her against him. He quirked an eyebrow. "Okay, so you're hard as a rock. You don't have to show off."

"I have a lot to *show* you." His voice was low and sexy.

"Then enough with the chitchat, big guy. Let's do this."

Nate abruptly stood, ripping a squeal from Jade. But he held on to her tightly, wrapping her legs around his waist as he carried her into the bedroom, kissing her passionately all the way.

Placing her on her feet, he took his damn time removing the rest of her clothing. But she made quick work of stripping him naked; it would be a crime to cover that body for a moment longer. He took her breath away every time she looked at him. Strong, toned, and that tattoo over his pec made him look badass.

She scrambled on the bed, and he followed her. He paused above her. She looked into his eyes, and for a moment she could see herself reflected in them. Her heart and soul shone back at her. Oh God, this was not good. She couldn't fall. Not for Nate. The man was leaving.

But when Nate placed his mouth on her breast and sucked in a nipple, her back arched off the bed and all coherent thoughts flew from her mind. He followed through with his promise of taking things slow. After paying her girls an equal amount of attention his lips moved down to her stomach, along her inner thighs, and back up. Only to start all over again until Jade was a quivering mess, panting and desperate for him like she'd never been before.

Finally, when he entered her, she burst into a thousand pieces, and Nate was right along with her, reaching their peak together.

Just before she drifted off to sleepy oblivion, the thought of the days of them being together soon ending entered her mind, and her heart ached.

Jade slowly came awake in the dark bedroom, the spot next to her in bed empty. Soft music floated in the air along with the smooth, sexy timbre of Nate's voice.

Getting out of bed, she threw on Nate's t-shirt and padded barefoot toward the beautiful sound. He wasn't in the living room, so she made her way to the kitchen, checking carefully around the doorway in case Nate was online with someone. She didn't want a repeat of the other night.

With his back to her, Nate sat on a kitchen stool with a guitar propped on his thigh. He was shirtless and wearing faded denim jeans, his hair tousled from her fingers. As he strummed the guitar, the muscles worked in his back. The sight stopped her heart.

She leaned her shoulder against the doorframe, enjoying the beautiful sounds coming from the man and his instrument. As she listened to the lyrics, a tingling sensation exploded across her body.

. . .

I close my eyes and picture you standing there.

Your touch is all I crave.

For you, I'd rip off my disguise and give up everything for a whisper of your love.

I'd give you the stars to make you smile.

Rattled by the words, she slowly backed out of the kitchen. Oh God, that song. So beautiful, so loving. But they were only words to him; he couldn't mean them. He was a songwriter—they made this stuff up all the time. But hearing them was like an arrow to the heart, because it meant so much more to her.

She held her palms to her chest. The pounding behind her ribs beat stronger and stronger until she thought her heart would explode. This was really, really bad. The man who sang like an angel but looked like a rock god had made her fall in love with him. And he would leave her. Just like the curse predicted.

Chapter 22

*N*ate penciled the last line down on the sheet of paper on the table. After making love to Jade, he couldn't fall asleep. Song lyrics kept swimming around his brain until he gave up on sleep and went into the kitchen to write them down. Never had his song writing flowed so freely. Inspiration poured onto the page.

Coming home to Brimland Point, away from the heaviness of his band, opened a new part of him. But if he were to be honest with himself, it wasn't his hometown getting his creative juices flowing, it was the woman. Having Jade as his muse changed his song writing to something deeper, more emotional. And it kind of scared the crap out of him. He didn't sing about love and commitment and happily ever after. But every song he wrote now had the same theme. And he liked it. Liked the way it made him feel.

A noise behind him had him turning around. Jade

stood dressed at the kitchen doorway. That wasn't how he'd left her. He'd left her asleep, naked, and thoroughly sated. The plan was to give her some time to recover and they'd start all over again. Would he ever get enough of her? He would have to, because once he left for New York it all had to end.

"I was about to come back to bed." After getting the song out of his head, exhaustion had hit. And the thought of sleeping with her in his arms was, after sex, the best way to end the day.

"I'm heading home. I've called a taxi to pick me up."

"Stay the night. You don't have school tomorrow. We can sleep in and spend the day in bed." And keep her there for days if he could.

He rose from the chair, walked to her, and reached out to pull her into his arms. But she stepped back out of reach. *What the fuck?*

"I have to get home to organize things for the substitute teacher. She needs to know what the kids are up to."

"Fuck that. Let Toby handle the substitute teacher. He's the one who's stopping you from working."

"Nate. I'm doing it for the children," she said. "I really should go."

He could tell by the set expression on her face he wouldn't change her mind. "Let me put on a shirt and I'll take you."

A car honked its horn outside.

"My taxi's already here. Goodnight, Nate."

What had turned Jade so cold? It was only an hour

ago she'd been fiery hot in his bed. He wasn't buying her bullshit excuse about getting school work ready for the substitute teacher. But he nodded, said goodnight, and watched her walk out the door.

As Nate sat back on the chair, Dorito woke up from his bed and wound his body around Nate's legs. Nate picked him up, let the cat rub his face along his bristly chin, and placed him on his lap. He'd grown rather fond of the little red furball.

There was another redhead he'd grown extremely fond of too, and he let her walk out the door. But what could he have done? It didn't look like she wanted to talk about what was bothering her.

He glanced down at the song he'd written. The intention was to write it and send it off to Roan Blake to sing. But it was too personal. Too much of Jade shone in the lyrics. This one he was keeping for himself.

The line *for you, I'd rip off my disguise and give up everything for a whisper of your love* sprang from off the page. It wasn't the first time he'd thought about giving it all away. He was serious about doing it, to take the attention off Jade so she could get back to her normal life. And in a perfect world, maybe they could share a love. A family. A life.

He ran his hand through his hair. He shouldn't think about unattainable things. By losing the disguise to be with Jade, he'd be letting down a lot of people. His band, the record company, fans…his father. And that was the crux of it all. The dream his father built for himself and wanted his son to follow would all be gone. The one piece that held him to his father would no longer connect them.

He had commitments and obligations to stick to, and he would see them through. Even if it meant a part of his soul got lost in the process. He had enough musical creativity with the band to keep him happy. And after playing his own stuff at Jovi's without the disguise, why couldn't he do the same in whatever city he was in?

Picking up his guitar, he brought it into the living room and put it away in its worn-out case. No one would ever know, and he'd have the best of both worlds. But that would still mean he couldn't promise Jade anything. Not love or commitment. Soon he'd be on the other side of the world touring most of the year. His chest tightened. In time, he'd get over her. He'd have to.

After getting the taxi driver to drop her off at the school to pick up her car, Jade drove around Brimland Point for an hour before deciding to go to Ava's house. Going home wasn't an option. She'd driven past, and after the story proclaiming her involvement with Nathan Harvey, the size of the paps camped on the lawn had doubled.

Didn't they have anything better to do? She didn't have the strength to push her way through them, especially when they ask her questions about their relationship. After the realization she was in love with Nate, she didn't want to accidentally blurt out anything they could twist into another article.

A cool sea breeze blew around her as she knocked on Ava's door, reminding her of Nate and the night in the ocean. She needed to push that memory aside.

Worried about the late hour, she'd messaged Ava, telling her that she was coming. Her friend, now in the late stages of pregnancy, hardly slept and messaged back that she'd be grateful for the visit.

Nick opened the door. Dressed only in long pajama pants, his chest was bare and his dark brown hair tousled. He smiled at her with startling blue eyes. God, her friends managed to tie down good-looking men. Jade had an extremely hot man of her own, but unfortunately, he was only temporary.

"Sorry, did I wake you?" Jade said as she followed him inside.

"No, just keeping Ava company until you arrived. She's feeling a little uncomfortable."

"Everything okay?" Jade asked with concern.

"She's been cleaning the house all day, and now she's exhausted but can't get comfortable enough to sleep." He gave her an *I don't know what to do* shrug.

"I should let her get some rest." Jade turned to leave, but Nick stopped her.

"No, don't go. She wants to see you. She won't sleep until she does."

"Are you sure?" Jade asked.

"Yes, I'm sure," came Ava's voice in the direction of the living room. "Stop talking about me behind my back and come in here so I can tell you everything myself. I'll be pissed if you make me get up."

"A little moody?" Jade whispered.

Nick's eyes widened. "God, don't say that to Ava, she'll bite your head off," he whispered back.

They moved into the living room where Ava was lying on the couch with multiple pillows propped behind her back. Jade sat on the chair opposite her friend.

"I've been calling you all day. I could have gone into labor and you wouldn't have known. Then if you'd missed it, it's your bad luck. Because I'm not doing this again." Ava tried crossing her arms over her chest but her belly got in the way.

Having the good sense to look chagrined, Jade said, "I'm sorry. I've had a full-on day. And I've told Nick to message me when the time comes."

Ava huffed. "Well, it was rude."

"I know. I'm sorry," she apologized again.

"I'll leave you two girls to talk. I'll be in the office if you need me." Nate bent and gave Ava a kiss on the lips, and her friend beamed like she was a teenager in love. It was still so weird seeing Ava smitten with a man.

Once Nick left Ava said, "I saw the article. The primary school teacher bagged the rock star, did she?"

"I'm not exactly a teacher anymore."

Ava frowned. "What do you mean?"

"Toby wasn't happy about the article. Parents were calling and complaining. It's not great seeing their children's teacher with her arse exposed for the world to see and flipping the bird."

"Toby fired you because of the article?"

"No, he put me on *leave* because a parent caught me kissing Nate in the hall after music lessons."

Ava shook her head. "God, Jade, for someone who's kept a relatively simple life, you sure turned it upside down. Toby can't be serious about putting you on leave. You're one of his best teachers."

"It wasn't easy for him. I understand he has to appease the parents. I'm supposed to be involved with a musician, but I'm seen kissing the music teacher. It looks bad."

"Your personal life is *personal*."

"Not when it's splashed in the tabloids. As a teacher, I have a certain image to uphold. And I haven't done so."

Ava rubbed her belly. "It still sucks."

Yeah, it did.

"How does Nate feel about all this?"

"He offered to give up his disguise so they'd leave me alone."

Ava's eyes widened. "Wow, that's a huge sacrifice. He must care a lot about you. Is this turning into something more than a fling?"

Jade's heart gave a little stutter. She'd done what she promised herself she wouldn't do—fall in love. But Nate didn't have the same feelings—he was just being honorable.

Jade averted her gaze and looked at a photo on a side table like it was the most fascinating thing she'd ever seen. "No, it's nothing like that. He just feels bad that I'm dealing with everything, and he wants to try to fix things."

"Jade…" Ava's tone told her she didn't believe her lie. "You like this guy, don't you? It's more than a fling."

She shook her head.

Ava pointed a finger at her and looked at her intensely. "Yes, you do. It's written all over your face. So what stage are you at? You like him? You more than like him? Or you *love* him?"

Jade bit her lip to stop from spilling the truth.

"Oh, Jade. You love him."

"But I didn't say—"

Ava's finger made a circling motion, and again, she said, "Written all over your face. You are always so bad at hiding your emotions."

Jade slumped in her chair. There was no point in continuing to deny it. Ava knew her too well. "I don't know what to do," Jade said.

"What do you mean? You tell him how you feel, and after what you told me, he probably feels the same way or he'd never offer to give up his identity."

"You're reading too much into it. I know he cares about me, nothing more than that. Besides, he'll be leaving soon. I can't let it turn into more, the curse would just ruin everything."

"For God's sake, enough about that stupid curse. I'm sick of hearing about it. Grow up and get over—" Ava sucked in a breath and clutched her belly.

Jade bounded off the chair and knelt by Ava's side. "Are you okay?" The comment stung, but she needed to push it aside for now and concentrate on her friend.

Ava breathed slow and deep before answering. "Yes, I'm good. I think it's one of those Braxton Hicks contractions." Jade must have had a confused expression on her face, because Ava explained, "They prepare the body for labor. I'm due in a week, so I think they've started."

"It looked strong. Are they supposed to be like that?"

"Hell if I know. I should have read more about them." She laughed, but then her face screwed up again and she cried out in pain.

"Nick!" Jade called, but he was already running down the hallway. He must have heard Ava.

He knelt next to Jade and grabbed Ava's hand. "Is it time?" His voice was panicked.

"I've either wet myself or my water broke." Ava cringed.

Both Nick and Jade looked toward Ava's crotch. A pool of liquid stained the couch.

Nick kissed Ava on the lips and smiled. "The baby's coming." Then he blew out a long breath and said again, but this time with an air of wonder, "The baby's coming."

Ava groaned, held her belly, and gritted her teeth. "Get the bag. We need to go to the hospital."

Nick sprang to his feet and raced back from where he came. In record time he was dressed and rolling a bag behind him, with car keys in hand.

After helping Ava off the couch, they carefully and slowly guided her outside. They had to stop twice so Ava could breathe through more contractions.

Finally, she was bundled into the car.

"I'll follow you to the hospital," Jade said.

"Can you call Lauren? My hands are shaking so much I'm not sure I can dial the number." He lifted his hand to prove it.

"Of course. Now go!" Jade pushed Nick toward the car as Ava clutched her belly in the seat.

Nick didn't waste any more time. He was off like a rocket.

Jade watched the car drive away, locked up the house, called Lauren, and followed them to the hospital.

Chapter 23

*D*awn broke through the waiting room's dirty windows, and pale golden light reflected off the sterile white walls as Jade blinked her eyes open. She must've dozed off. Stretching, she glanced over at Lauren who was curled up on an old, brown sofa.

It had been hours since they'd last seen Nick. He'd come out for a minute to give them an update on Ava's condition and dashed away before they could ask any questions. Now, with no more information, Jade worried there might be complications.

Before Jade could find a nurse to hopefully get an update, Nick came bounding into the room.

"It's a girl!" he announced with excitement as dark smudges lined the bottoms of his eyes.

Jade jumped from the chair. Lauren sprang awake and got up too.

"A girl. How wonderful." Lauren congratulated and hugged Nick.

"Did everything go okay? How's Ava?" Jade asked as she too hugged him.

Nick scrubbed his hands over his face and shook his head with an expression of wonder, like what happened had just sunk in. "They're both great. Healthy. Perfect. Oh my God. The baby is beautiful. And Ava…" His voice cracked, and he cleared his throat. "She was a warrior. I'm never gonna complain about the man flu again."

"There's another baby in the group. Congratulations, man," Lauren's husband Jack said as he walked into the waiting room, holding their son Ryan on his hip. He slapped Nick on the back with his free hand.

"What are you doing here?" Lauren rushed to their side.

"Mama, Mama," Ryan squealed as he reached his chubby, little arms for his mother. She didn't hesitate to take him.

"He woke up super freaking early and wouldn't go back to sleep. I thought I'd come here and see how things were going."

Lauren kissed Ryan on the neck, making him giggle, then placed a soft kiss on Jack's lips.

"Can we see them?" Jade asked Nick.

"Yes, she's been moved from the delivery suite into her room. But it can only be a quick visit. She's exhausted."

They followed him down a couple of corridors and entered Ava's room. She was tucked up in bed, cradling her baby in her arms, beaming with love and pride as she gazed at her bundle.

They all rushed to her side, taking turns to get a closer

look. A little, chubby face with thick, black hair slept in her mother's arms with no idea how much she would be loved. Not only by her parents but by all the people in the room.

Jack carefully held Ryan so he could have a look at the newborn, then said, "Buddy, meet your new girlfriend. Her daddy's rich, so you're set for life."

"You can forget about it. My little girl is not allowed out until she's thirty-five." Nick threw Jack a disgusted glare. "Point your kid somewhere else."

They all chuckled.

"Do we have a name yet?" Jade asked.

"We've decided on Adriana," Ava answered as she gently caressed the baby's cheek.

After they all had a good look and a quick cuddle, Lauren wandered around the room. She opened the door that led to the bathroom and peeked inside, she looked in a cupboard, she even glanced under the bed.

"What are you looking for?" Ava asked.

"I'm searching for your glam-squad, because there is no way in hell you can look that good after hours of labor and giving birth," Lauren grumbled. "After I had Ryan, I looked like crap. And you…" She waved a hand in her direction. "…don't."

Ava laughed.

Jack put his arm around Lauren's shoulders. "You looked beautiful too. You always do."

She smiled and pressed herself against him, tilting her face up for a kiss.

The room was so full of love, it smothered Jade until

her lungs squeezed and she could barely breathe. This was what she wanted. What she'd never have. And even though she was happy for her friends and their new families, she needed to get out of there before she screamed *it's not fair!*

"I'm going so you can rest." It surprised Jade how calm her voice sounded while she shook on the inside.

"Yes, we better get going too and get Ryan back to bed," Lauren said as she lovingly looked at her son who'd fallen asleep on Jack's shoulder.

They said their goodbyes and left the room.

When they were outside Lauren asked, "Want to come over and have a coffee?"

"Thanks, but I'm going home."

Lauren looked intently at Jade. "Are you okay?"

Jade's smile felt stiff on her face, but she hoped she didn't alert her friend to how she was really feeling. "I'm tired, that's all. I need to sleep."

"It has been a long night. I might join Ryan for a nap too." Lauren gave Jade a quick hug. "I'll call you later."

Over the weekend, Nate Facetimed his band and they made plans for the next leg of the tour and went over the new songs they wanted to include on the album. He didn't know how much longer he could stay in Brimland Point. Mike was eager to get the new tracks recorded and ready to go. And more than once told him he should be back already.

The band had played a few smaller shows again with Jimmy singing lead vocals. And word was getting around that Nathan Harvey had left the band. He'd done three phone interviews explaining he hadn't left and was working on new material for the tour. Questions regarding Jade was the number one topic, but Nate shut them down before they could go any further. If they wanted an interview with him, they had to leave her out of it.

He'd gone two days without seeing her, and it had been the longest days of his life. Who knew he'd look forward to seeing her bubbly personality, her vibrant smile, and her bright, curly hair every day?

She'd gotten under his skin, worked her way into his —no, he wouldn't say heart. But she'd made an impact in his life. Well, his life in Brimland Point. When he left, it would be the end. Maybe it was for the best they spent some time apart. Better to not get too attached. It would only make leaving harder. His gut clenched. It might already be too late.

***

Monday afternoon Nate tuned some instruments in the hall, getting them ready for class. After Toby had asked Jade to take time off, Nate had assumed the lessons would be over too. But Toby wanted them to continue; the kids were enjoying them.

Nate actually looked forward to the classes too. He loved seeing their smiling faces when they learned a new chord or verse of a song. They concentrated so hard, pushed through the frustration of when it didn't work out, until they played awesome music. Who knew teaching kids could be so fun and rewarding? The only thing missing was Jade. It wouldn't be the same without her.

As he finished getting the equipment ready, the kids walked into the hall in single file. They didn't run in like wild animals to grab the instrument of their choice as they normally did. No one made a sound. Nate frowned. Something wasn't right.

A stern-looking woman in her sixties followed them. Her hair was pulled back in a severe bun, and she wore a black blouse buttoned to her neck with a frilly, white collar. A heavy burgundy skirt passed her knees, revealing thick, gray pantyhose. This woman looked like a scary nanny. Something straight out of the movies.

When the kids made a slight noise, she clapped her hands loudly. "Children, the next person to make a sound will sit out of the class." She peered at every child with pursed lips. When no one moved, just stared wide-eyed at the teacher, she said, "Now sit down *quietly* and wait for instructions from Mr. Miller."

Holy crap, not only were the kids scared, he was shaking a little in his boots too.

"Mr. Miller, I'm Mrs. Rich. I'll be supervising the lessons while Ms. Brennan is away." Without waiting for any kind of reply, she pulled a chair in front of the kids and gave them another warning glare.

Why the hell did Toby ask this horrible woman to

supervise a class that was meant to be fun? Nate hoped she didn't suck the joy out of it. With no other choice, he started the lesson.

After only ten minutes, Nate knew this would be a disaster. Mrs. Rich already had Lachlan sitting in a corner because he played a few notes more than the rest of the class after the song ended, which she considered *noise*. And Suzie's lips trembled when Mrs. Rich told her that her guitar skills needed big improvement.

This would be the longest hour of his life.

———

Jade stood at the entrance of the hall and stared at the somber-looking class. She'd stopped by the school to drop off work for the substitute teacher when she heard the music coming from the hall. When she entered, instead of the happy, noisy music that normally filled the room, a depressing atmosphere was in its place. A lot like Jade's mood.

She'd been asked to stop teaching, but the music lessons, which she fought for, were still running. Sure, she was happy the kids still had them, but while her life was falling apart, everyone else's kept moving on. Even Nate's.

She turned to leave but Lachlan, who sat on the floor not taking part in the lesson, spotted her.

"Ms Brennan!" he squealed, got up, bolted for her, and wrapped skinny, little arms around her waist.

When the other kids saw what was happening, they

too called out her name, dropped their instruments, and surrounded her.

"Children. Enough!" Mrs. Rich—aka Mrs. Witch, what Jade and some of the other staff liked to call her—clapped her hands and yelled, "Come here at once." She pointed at the floor near her feet like she was calling a dog to come and sit.

The children dropped their heads and dragged their feet to her.

"That kind of behavior is unacceptable. Your lesson is over. Line up in single file and leave the hall. You can wait for your parents outside. If I hear a peep out of anyone, you'll have lunch time detention tomorrow. Is that clear?"

"Yes, Mrs. Rich," they mumbled as they trudged out of the room with Mrs. Witch following them.

Nate shuddered. "She's enough to give any kid nightmares. In fact, I don't think I'll sleep well tonight. How does Toby let her teach these poor kids?"

"She works in the library. She doesn't take classes."

"Thank God for that." Then he reached out to her. "I've missed you."

Stepping away, she said, "Don't. Anyone could walk in."

"What more can they do to you? They've already taken your job."

And Nate had taken her heart, and there was nothing she could do about that either. "I'm on temporary leave. I don't want to do anything to make it permanent."

Nate blew out a breath. "I still can't believe Toby did

this to you. You should teach at this school and supervise music lessons. Not that dragon woman."

"And yet you're still teaching like nothing has changed," Jade said in a sharp tone.

"What's that supposed to mean?" His eyes narrowed.

She shook her head. "Nothing. I should go."

Nate grasped her arm before she could turn to leave. "I know this is hard on you, so if you want me to cancel the lessons, I will."

The kids loved music. She couldn't take that away from them because she was feeling sorry for herself. "No, I don't want you to cancel the class."

"Then what is it? Talk to me." Concern lined his face.

She wanted to tell him her friends married the men of their dreams and were having beautiful babies. But she'd never have the one man she'd let herself fall in love with and have a life like that.

Instead, she said, "Really, it's nothing. It surprised me to see the music lessons still going, that's all. I feel a little sad that I'm not involved anymore. When I get back, we can make them exciting again. Hopefully, Mrs. Rich won't scare the kids away by then."

Nick dropped his gaze for a beat then scrubbed the back of his neck.

"But you'll be gone." God, how stupid she was. She knew he wouldn't be here that long. "I'll find another music teacher."

"I have a few contacts. I'll call around and see who I can get to help," he said.

Not once had he suggested he might want to stay. He

was leaving. He told her so from the start. Why would she think he'd ever change his mind? He never gave her the impression he would stay, especially for her.

She wasn't able to stand in front of him a minute longer, because the chances of her saying something she might regret, like begging him not to go, was strong. So she put on the best smile she could spread on her face. "That would be great. Thank you." She flicked out her wrist and pretended to look at the time. "I have to go."

He stopped her again by holding onto her arm. The warmth of his hand turned her skin on fire. "Have dinner with me," he said. "Come to my house and I'll cook."

"Sorry, I can't. Ava had her baby. I want to visit them." Which was a lie; she was going home, putting on her oldest and most comfortable pajamas, and watching old episodes of *Buffy*. A tub of hazelnut chocolate ice cream was on the menu.

"Mother and baby doing okay?" he asked.

"Yes, they're perfect." Her heart squeezed again over the fact she would never experience that kind of love with her own husband and baby. She pulled her arm free and immediately felt the loss. "Bye, Nate."

"I'll be home if you change your mind," he said.

With a quick nod, she spun on her heels and rushed from the room.

Chapter 24

*J*ade sat curled up on the couch with an empty tub of hazelnut chocolate ice cream. She'd dropped a spoonful on her pajama top, and then made a big, brown mess while trying to clean it up.

Like she'd planned, she was watching *Buffy*, but even the vampire slayer couldn't have the man she wanted. If she had sex with Angel, he'd turn evil. And Angel, being a vampire, would never give her a normal life, so he dumped her and left!

Story of my life. Jade couldn't watch Buffy's heartache a moment longer—she had enough of her own pain to deal with—and she flicked it off.

As she rose from the couch to go in search of more ice cream a knock sounded at the door. She paused. She wasn't expecting anyone. Now that the media finally got sick of watching her uneventful house and a famous actor checked themselves into rehab, they'd packed up and moved on. It would piss her off if some journalist was still hanging around and had the audacity to come to the door. Maybe if she ignored it, whoever it was would go away.

The knock sounded again, and a muffled voice called through the door. "Jade, open up."

Nate. She'd told him she wouldn't be home. Why would he come over?

She wasn't emotionally prepared to see him. Or dressed for that matter. How could she open the door and pretend her life was wonderful when every time she looked at him her heart died a little? If she ignored him, he'd think she wasn't home then leave.

"Jade, open up. Why are you just standing there?"

What the hell? That door was solid timber; did he have x-ray vision?

Then she saw a dark silhouette at her window. She'd forgotten to close the blinds, and he had his hands to the glass, peeking through the venetians.

Crap! Now she had to let him in.

She trudged to the door and opened it. Nate stood on the veranda wearing faded jeans and a gray t-shirt that clung to his chest. His hair was a little tousled, and he was sporting some sexy afternoon stubble. He held a pizza, and her mouth watered. But not because of the cheesy aroma coming from the box.

Frowning at her, he said, "Were you ignoring me?"

Jade nibbled her bottom lip and shook her head. "No."

A dubious eyebrow rose. "Yes, I think you were."

She capitulated at his suspicious perusal. "Only because I look like a mess." She pointed to the chocolate stain on her Bugs Bunny pajamas. *And because my heart can't cope.* But she kept that to herself.

"It's nothing I haven't seen before. You seem to wear a lot of your food." He smirked, referring to the mess on her shirt when he came to the school for the first time. Thankfully, he'd bought her excuse.

"How did you know I was home?" she asked.

"I didn't for sure. It was getting late, I didn't think you'd be with Ava all this time."

Jade averted her gaze for a beat, hoping her face didn't give away the lie.

"I bought a pizza and took my chances. Am I going to stand outside all night, or can I come in?" he asked.

She moved away from the door and gestured for him to enter. "Put the box on the coffee table. I'll get napkins."

In the kitchen, she took a moment to take a few deep breaths. She hadn't planned on seeing Nate tonight. And now that she wasn't teaching at school anymore, she had no reason to see him again. She was hoping the old saying *out of sight out of mind* would kick in. How was she supposed to forget him when he showed up at her door with pizza? A hot guy with food was too good to turn down.

After a few moments to calm her racing heart, she found napkins and went back into the living room. Nate sat on the couch with the remote in his hand. He'd turned the TV back on.

"She's in love with a vampire?" he asked. "What kind of dumb show is this?"

Jade held a hand to her chest. "Don't criticize a classic."

"You watch this?"

"And love it. So be careful what you say," she playfully warned.

Laughing, he turned the TV off and opened the box of pizza.

Jade sat in an armchair on the opposite side of the coffee table to Nate, not trusting herself to sit too close. The closer he was, the more her body wanted to climb all over him, and that would not help in her crusade of forgetting him. When he left, so would all the feelings she had for him. It would be that simple. It had to be, or she'd collapse in a heap.

For now, she'd enjoy the pizza and pretend it was only friendship between them. Well, it was on his part. So as long as she kept it that way on her end, she'd eventually believe it. *Yeah, right.*

They sat in silence as they devoured the first few slices. Then Nate wiped his mouth with a napkin, slumped back on the couch, and said, "Jade, what's wrong?"

Jade still had a bite of cheesy goodness in her mouth. At the moment nothing was wrong. How could there be when she was eating her favorite food? She pointed to her mouth to show she couldn't speak.

He waited for her to finish and asked again before she could take another bite. *Sneaky.*

"The problem is, there isn't enough cheese," she answered.

"That's because you're wearing most of it on your top." He pointed to her chest. "I swear you need a bib when you eat." He laughed.

Jade scooped up the melted mess with her finger and scraped it on the edge of the box. "I was saving it for later."

He laughed harder.

God, she would miss that sound. *No, don't go there. Just enjoy the night like two friends. Only friends.* She needed to keep reminding herself.

When he stopped laughing, he pinned her with a searching stare. "I know something *is* wrong, and it's not the cheese."

He got off the couch, walked around the coffee table, and squeezed down next to her in the large chair. Their legs touched from hip to knee, and her body grew tingly and warm. She tried shuffling away as much as she could to put space between them, but he slid his arm over her shoulders, anchoring her on the seat.

Placing a finger under her chin, he turned her face to him. "You can talk to me."

He'd said the same thing in the hall earlier in the day. She'd avoided telling him then what was on her mind. But with the way his gaze watched her with concern she wanted to give him something.

"I'm feeling a little sorry for myself. It's nothing to worry about."

"Why are you feeling sorry for yourself? Is it because

the music lessons are continuing? I told you'd I'd stop them—"

"No, it's not that. Well, a small part of it is. But I want the kids to have the lessons. I'm sad I can't be part of it."

"But there's more," he prompted.

Ava had said Jade couldn't hide her emotions, but hopefully she could mask what she was feeling with him. To stop any signs of her love showing, she chanted in her mind: *Just friends. Just friends. Good friends. Friends with benefits.* No! Not friends with benefits.

With his hand brushing in circular motions over her shoulder, she was finding it hard to concentrate. She again tried to wiggle away, but he held on tight.

"My best friends are married with wonderful husbands. They've both had beautiful, healthy babies, and I'm a little envious. They have it all. And all I'll ever have is Dorito, who I love, but it's not the same as my own human family."

"You can have all that too."

"I can't. The curse—"

"Let go of that damn curse and you *will* find love. Some guy would be lucky to have you and *never* leave."

Some guy. Not Nate. Her heart dropped to her stomach. If there was one man she would maybe take the chance with, it would be Nate, but he didn't want to be *that guy.*

"I wish it could be me," he whispered.

Wait…did she say that out loud? Or were her feelings, which she'd tried to hide, written all over her face?

He removed his arm from around her shoulders, shifted in the chair, and wiped the palms of his hands on his jeans. "Mike has been nagging me to get back to New York. We've been working on some music he wants to record before we head out on tour again."

"When do you leave?" She could tell by his solemn expression he wasn't going to tell her he was staying.

"Friday."

Her heart squeezed, and she sucked in a sharp breath. "So soon?"

"I've found someone to replace me for the music lessons. I've passed her information on to Toby."

Did he think she cared about that? He was leaving in a matter of days. She'd never see him again. Except if she watched the music channels and caught his latest video. But the rock star wasn't the man she loved. The man she loved was leaving just like she knew he would. But she didn't want to show him how much it hurt.

"That's great. I look forward to working with her." Her voice rose to a forced cheery pitch, and he frowned.

"I'd stay longer, but the band needs me. I've been away longer than I'd planned."

"You have a job to do. You must be eager to get back on stage." She bounded off the chair, but before she took two steps, Nate held her by the wrist, pulling her back down.

"I hate the thought of leaving you." His eyes bore into hers.

Then don't leave, she wanted to yell.

"This next leg of the tour goes for two months. Then I

have another break, and I'll come back. This doesn't have to end here."

"How long is your break, and what happens after that?" she asked.

"We have a six-week break. Then a few shows for charity to put on in Italy, Spain, and England."

"How long will you be away doing these events?" Jade asked, forcing the tremor from her voice.

"A month. Maybe longer."

She'd heard this all before. When she was a little girl and she would sit with her father before he left to go on flights around the world, she'd ask him similar questions. At first, he'd be gone two days, then two weeks, then a month. Until eventually he never came home.

She couldn't go through that again. Nate might think they could make it work, but she knew better. Eventually he'd never come back. Only moments ago, he'd said *some guy* would be lucky to have her. He wasn't thinking long-term. He was only thinking until his next break, and then he'd move on.

"Don't make plans you're not sure you can keep. A long-distance relationship is hard work."

"We could try."

Struggling with the thoughts in her head and the emotions in her heart, her head told her to put distance between them. Show him the door and tell him to have a nice life. Her heart wanted to hold on to him for every last second; she'd deal with the broken pieces when he left.

She wouldn't get many moments like this with him

again, so why deny herself as much time as possible with him?

"No. It would never work." And the curse would only end it anyway. "You're here now, let's make the most of the time we have left," she said and slid her hand along his chest.

Nate didn't argue the case, because deep down he must know she was right. Instead, his eyes heated as she trailed her palm down the length of his torso. He sucked in a sharp breath when her fingertips slid into the waistband of his jeans.

Lowering his mouth to hers, he paused before claiming her lips. She looked into his eyes, desire beaming from them. And for a second, just before he kissed her, she thought she saw something more. A need for her that went beyond lust. Her heart stopped. No, it couldn't be more. Her mind must be playing tricks on her. And as his hands skimmed her with feather-light strokes along her body, turning her into a quivering mess, all intelligent thoughts left the building.

After, as they lay sated and panting on the couch—arms and legs tangled—she breathed in his woodsy, soapy scent, wanting to take every part of him in. And it was then her chest seized and lungs tightened. She'd been wrong. She'd never be able to pick up the pieces of her broken heart when he left because it had already shattered.

Chapter 25

A suitcase lay open on Nate's unmade bed. He piled his clothes inside, flipped it closed, and wheeled it into the living room, his guitar propped on the wall in its case ready to go. That's all he had. The furniture in the house was part of the rental.

Dorito laid curled up in a ball in a sunny spot of the room, fast asleep. The little fur ball had grown on him. He'd miss him.

The cat wasn't the only thing he would miss. He loved being back in his hometown with his grandmother and Toby. Sure, he was close with his band mates, but nothing felt better than being surrounded by the people who truly knew you. His band mostly saw him as Nathan Harvey, not Nate Miller. They didn't know the real person.

And then Jade had burst into his life like a ball of fiery light, not giving a shit about his stage persona. And because he didn't have to hide that part of himself, it made him feel more *normal* than he ever had in his life. Too bad he couldn't stay longer to see where they could take their relationship. But with her believing in curses, and with the amount of travel he did, could they have made it work?

He'd meant it when he suggested they could try, but the more time he had to think, the more he realized Jade was right. He shouldn't make plans he wasn't sure he could keep when he was on the road most of the time. It was selfish to ask Jade to wait for him when he happened to have a month off once in a while. A clean break would be best for both. A sharp pain sliced through his chest, and he leaned against the wall. God, leaving her was going to kill him.

These last few days Jade had been different, not her usual bubbly self. He put it down to the stress of not working and the turmoil he'd thrown into her life. He hated that he'd caused her so much trouble and couldn't fix it. Even though she kept telling him she was fine, she'd lost the happy spark in her eyes.

They'd spent a lot of their limited time together wrapped in each other's arms. Their lovemaking started out fast and frantic, like they couldn't wait a second to get their hands on each other. Then continued on to something slower, like they didn't want it to end. Each day it got harder and harder to drag himself away from her. Today would be the hardest. He'd drop off Dorito and say goodbye. Shoving his fingers through his hair, he pushed away from the wall and swore.

Finally, he had found someone he could picture

spending his life with, only for it to be impossible. He couldn't give her what she needed. Or give himself the life he wanted. The obligation to his father was what his life was about. He'd promised him he'd never let his music die.

He walked into the kitchen. Dorito must have known he was about to get food because he followed him, stretching as he peered into his bowl.

Nate opened a can of tuna and spooned it out for the hungry cat. "I'll see you later, buddy. I'll be taking you to your new home."

The cat devoured his meal, not giving Nate an ounce of attention as he left the house.

***

Nate found Toby sitting in Fi-Fi's kitchen, a steaming cup of coffee on the table in front of him. She was showing him something on her phone.

When Nate first left Brimland Point with his band, Toby promised he'd keep an eye on Fi-Fi. All these years later, he still dropped by.

"Hi, honey." His grandmother beamed a bright, pink lip smile. "I was just getting Toby's opinion on what stripper shoes I should buy."

Toby stared at him with horror in his eyes.

"You'll never be able to walk into a strip club again without thinking of Fi-Fi and her shoes." Nate laughed.

Toby dropped his head in his hands.

"These are for pole dancing, not stripping. Get your minds out of the gutter." Fi-Fi huffed.

Nate wanted to scrub the image of his grandmother pole dancing out of his mind, and judging by the look on Toby's face, he did too. "I hear there's a great line dancing class at the Leisure Centre. Why don't you give that a go?"

Fi-Fi slapped a hand on a hip covered in leopard print spandex. "Why the hell would I want to line dance with a bunch of old people?"

Some would probably be a lot younger than her. But Nate kept that to himself. "Just a suggestion," he said, sitting at the table next to Toby.

"You heading off in the morning?" Toby asked.

"Yep. I fly out at seven."

"I'm going to miss you." His grandmother slid her hand across the table and squeezed his. "It's wonderful having you home for longer than five minutes. I actually thought you might stay for good."

He raised a brow. "You did? Why?"

"Because you were playing music you loved and your face beams with joy whenever you talk about it."

"I was only playing in a bar." But it did make him happy.

"And drawing in a decent crowd," Toby added.

"It was nothing important." The sinking feeling in his gut told him differently.

"And what about the teacher you're seeing, is that nothing important? Were you only playing around with her too?" Fi-Fi asked.

Toby threw him a serious look. One that said *you*

better not have been fucking around with my friend for the fun and giggles.

"Not with Jade, she means a lot to me," Nate answered.

"Well, do something about it," his grandmother said as if she didn't understand what the problem was.

"There's nothing I can do. I'm on the road too much for a successful relationship."

"Then stop going on the road. How many times do I need to tell you that band is making you miserable? *Home* is making you happy. And that includes playing your own music, even if it is in a small pub. It's not like you need the money. And a beautiful woman who you've spent every minute you can with has put the biggest smile on your face and a spring in your step. If those aren't good enough reasons to stay, I don't know what is. Stop trying to walk in your father's shoes."

"I promised him, Fi-Fi."

"He should never have made you promise to give your life away. He was my son and I love him and miss him terribly, but I can tell you he'd become selfish and conceited and wanted the world to revolve around him. Answer me this." She leaned forward and peered into his eyes. "If your father had never made you make that promise, if you could have any life you wanted, what would you be doing?"

Nate squirmed in his seat. If he lied, Fi-Fi would spot it a mile away. Like she always did.

"I'd be playing my own music, even writing songs for

other artists." The few he'd sent away were getting great airplay. And he'd been asked for more.

"Then follow *your* dream," she urged.

"It's not as simple as that."

His grandmother slumped back in her chair. "You're the only one who's making things complicated."

Nate couldn't listen to his grandmother's lecture any longer. He'd heard it all before. Although he'd never admitted it out loud, he'd rather be playing his own music. That, he only just recently discovered. And the part about Jade was new too. Did his grandmother think it was easy for him to leave her? But he had to do what was best for them both.

He said his goodbyes to Fi-Fi. It was always hard leaving her. Even though she was a fit seventy-nine-year-old, she *was* getting older, and he didn't know how many more times he'd get to see her. But by the way she was going, she'd probably outlive him.

"I'll walk you out," Toby said as he headed for the door.

Once outside, they stood by Nate's rental car.

"Are you sure you need to leave?" Toby asked.

"You're not going to start with me too, are you? I've heard enough from Fi-Fi."

"What about Jade, how's she taking it?"

Nate had put her quietness down to the stress of the last few days, the paparazzi, the newspaper article, and being on leave. But maybe it had something to do with him too. He knew it wasn't just a fling for her, no matter what she'd said at the start. It hadn't been a fling for him either. He genuinely cared for her. Leaving wouldn't be easy.

"Watch out for her for me, will you? And give her back her fucking job."

"You should watch out for her yourself." Toby sounded pissed. "You promised me you wouldn't mess around with her feelings. And I told you if you hurt her, you'd be dealing with me. Do I have to kick your arse?"

"I'd like to see you try." Now Nate was pissed. Why was everyone on his back? He had a job to do—commitments. No one seemed to care that leaving was cutting him too.

"I could kick your arse from here to New York," Toby grumbled. "Tell me, am I going to find Jade a broken mess?"

Maybe he should let Toby kick his arse. Beat him up so badly he couldn't feel a thing anymore. But he knew that even if his body was numb, his heart would still ache.

"Honestly, I don't know. But if she's feeling anything like I am at the moment, it isn't good." Nate's shoulders slumped.

"Do you love her?" Toby's voice lost some of its heat.

His heart thumped at the question. *Did he?* What he felt was something stronger than he'd ever felt for any woman.

When Nate didn't answer, Toby blew out a long breath, clearly taking his silence as confirmation. "Then make it work with her."

"Even if I wanted to, she's so caught up in that curse she wouldn't let it happen."

"If you stay, I'm sure you could convince her it's all bullshit," Toby suggested.

Could he stay and let his father's legacy go? But what if Jade couldn't let go of her beliefs—then what?

"At least think about it," Toby said.

"Okay, I will."

Chapter 26

*T*hursday night dinner at Jade's mother's house was a monthly occurrence. One that Jade didn't feel up to, but she knew if she didn't attend, her mum would whinge about not making an effort for the family. Although Jade wasn't sure how her mother could complain since Jade popped over all the time. Except for the last few days. She'd avoided coming past because she hadn't told her mum she'd been put on leave.

With no job to go to, she'd cleaned her place from top to bottom, ironed the pile of clothes that had been sitting in the laundry for months, did some grocery shopping, and briefly spent time with Ava, Nick, and baby Adriana.

Usually, Jade looked forward to her mother's cooking and spending time with her siblings. But today, she dragged heavy legs inside the house. She attributed her lethargy to a busy day and not because Nate was leaving in the morning.

Smells of a roast drifted through the house, and she

followed the scent into the kitchen. Her mother was by the sink washing lettuce, and Kaitlyn was setting the table with only three place settings.

"Hi, Ma." Jade kissed her on the cheek. "Where's Connor?"

"Hi, sweetheart. He got called into work."

"That's a shame." She lied because she didn't know if she could look him in the eye quite yet after getting busted making out in public again. She loved her brother, but she could do without the disapproving glare he would aim at her over dinner.

While their mother's back was turned, Kaitlyn winked at Jade and whispered, "How was your make-out session in the car?"

Jade shook her head, pretending she couldn't hear what her sister was saying.

"Do you really want me to repeat the question louder?" This time Kaitlyn didn't whisper.

"What question?" Their mother looked over her shoulder at them.

"Nothing," Jade said and threw her sister a dirty look.

Their mother wiped her hands on a dish towel and focused her attention on Jade. "What's wrong, sweetheart? You look sad."

"I do?"

Her mother nodded.

It would seem her emotions were out there for the world to see. Thankfully, Nate was too blind to notice. There was no point denying she'd seen better days, but how much did she tell them?

"Toby had to put me on annual leave." Needing to do something, she grabbed a knife and chopping board and cut cucumbers for the salad.

"What? Why?" Her mother frowned.

Jade scraped the cucumbers from the board into a bowl and started on the tomatoes. "Because parents were complaining about the article online. The one with my arse in the air and me flipping the bird."

"I can see why that could upset some parents, but surely they can understand that these people have been harassing you?" her mother snapped as she took the lamb from the oven and placed it on the counter. The scent of rosemary and garlic filled the kitchen. "I thought Toby had more sense than to be dictated to by parents who don't know the full facts. I'm disappointed in him. How long are you on leave?"

"Indefinitely," Jade answered.

"*Indefinitely!* How can he do this to you?" Her mother huffed.

"It's not Toby's fault. He tried really hard to support me. But then…" Jade bit her lip and flicked her gaze at Kaitlyn who sat on the edge of her seat, looking eager to hear the rest.

"And then what?" they both asked.

Paying close attention to putting the salad together, she said, "One afternoon after music lessons, a parent walked in on Nate and I kissing."

Jade's mother sucked in a quick breath.

"It doesn't look good for a primary school teacher to be involved with two different men at the same time."

"But they're not," Jade's mother pointed out.

"We know that, and Toby knows that, but no one else does. To calm everyone down, he thought it would be best if I lie low for a while."

"I still don't like how he's holding you to blame for something out of your control." Her mother sniffed.

"I talked to the paparazzi. I shouldn't have."

"Those leeches have been hounding you. I don't know how they live with themselves making money from innocent people." She sliced into the lamb with a bit too much force.

"Here, Ma, let me do that." Kaitlyn took the knife from her hand before she hurt herself.

"They've left the house now, so hopefully they've forgotten about me and Nate."

"What's been happening with him anyway?" Kaitlyn asked as she placed the roast on the table. "Besides...you know." She smirked.

Jade rolled her eyes.

They all sat at the table and passed around the plates of food. Finally, her mother said, "Well, are you going to answer your sister?"

There was no way she would tell her mother about getting busted by Connor making out in the car. It was bad enough her mum knew she'd been skinny-dipping. This would surely give her a heart attack. It surprised Jade that Connor and his big mouth hadn't run to tell on her.

"There's nothing much to say. He helped me out with music lessons." She shrugged. "That's all." And she'd fallen in love.

"You were making more than just *music* together," Kaitlyn said with a sly smile. Jade knew exactly what she was suggesting.

"After your…" Jade's mother cleared her throat. "…beach incident, are the two of you in a relationship? Maybe he's the one you can finally settle down with."

Jade nearly choked on the meat she was in the process of swallowing. Coughing a couple of times, she then took a sip of water. "No, Ma, I'm not settling down with him or anyone. You know why."

Her mother slapped her napkin on the table and gave Jade a stern stare. "This curse business used to be a bit of fun. You know—that couple broke up, it must be the Brennan curse. A joke. But you're taking it too far."

"But—"

"I haven't finished." She pointed a finger at Jade. "You're letting it come between you and your happiness. And you deserve the best life. You look sad, and it's not all because of your job. There's more to it, and I'll put my money on Nate. We thought you'd snap out of that nonsense when you fell in love."

"I'm not in love," she lied.

Her mother stared her down without saying a word.

"Okay." She could never lie to her mother when she gave her that look. "I might have some strong feelings…"

Again, the look.

"Fine." She threw her hands in the air. "I fell in love. But nothing can happen."

"Because of the curse." Her mother huffed.

"Yes."

"Have you told him how you feel?"

"There's no point. He's leaving in the morning. I can't stop him." A cold tightness squeezed her chest.

"If you love him, you need to tell him," her mother encouraged.

"He never planned on staying." She bit her bottom lip to stop it from trembling.

"He may surprise you and change his mind if he knows how you feel." Her mother placed a hand on her heart. "Or, as much as it would kill me, you could go with him."

Jade smiled. "Don't worry, I'm not leaving Brimland Point. My job is here—well, that's if Toby lets me come back. It would never work even if I went with him. The curse would see to that."

"Enough with the stupid curse! It isn't real," her mother snapped.

"What about all the broken relationships in our family? They've been real. Liz's fiancé and her younger sister Melissa's boyfriend, Kaitlyn's husband Phil, and…dad."

Jade's mother dropped her elbows on the table and placed her head in her hands. "Liz's fiancé was a jerk, he did her a favor. Melissa was only eighteen when she dated that boy, and he wasn't much older. They were too young for a relationship. And Phil…" Her eyes flicked to Kaitlyn.

Kaitlyn blew out a breath then blurted, "Phil was gay."

"I knew it!" Jade yelled. "No straight guy quotes from

the movie *Legally Blonde* and performs the bend-and-snap like a pro."

"You knew? Why didn't you say anything? You could have saved me two years of wondering why he rarely wanted sex." She made a cringing face when her mother sighed. "Sorry, Ma."

"I hoped I was wrong," Jade said.

"See, he didn't leave Kaitlyn, he was gay. They shouldn't have gotten married in the first place," her mother added.

"What about dad? He left." Heaviness sat like a rock on Jade's chest.

Her mother slumped in her chair. "*I* left him."

Jade's mouth fell open, and even Kaitlin look surprised. "That's not true."

"It is."

Shaking her head, Jade said, "No, he kept leaving for trips until he never came back home."

"That's because I told him not to. Our marriage was over. I put an end to it."

They'd never talked about why their father left. Jade had assumed the family curse was to blame. She didn't know her mother was the one to walk away. She thought they were in love.

Her mother continued. "As you know, I fell pregnant with Connor while we were dating. Your father wanted to do the right thing and get married. We probably shouldn't have—we were too young—but I'll never regret it, because then I had you two girls. We tried to make our marriage work for you kids, but it was only making us miserable. Your father wasn't happy about divorcing, but I didn't want you kids growing up around two people who would probably eventually hate each other."

Jade and Kaitlin both slumped back in their chair, looking at their mother with shocked expressions.

"Wow," Jade said while her insides shook with the news.

"I never thought you included your father in your list, but there really isn't a curse. I would never have made fun about it all these years if I'd known what you believed. We should have explained things better when we separated. It was a hard time, and we thought we were shielding you from the painful details." Her mother's eyes filled with tears. "I'm sorry I've ruined your chances of finding love."

"But the diary at Granny's house…it's all written in there." Jade was still unconvinced.

"There's a box in Granny's attic filled with old diaries and stories about many things your ancestor wrote about. I remember reading one about how she'd cursed the men in someone's family to be born with scales because the fisherman wouldn't give her free fish. No one is walking around with fish scales. There were many more stories like it, and none of them were true."

Jade clasped her trembling hands on her lap. Not true? For most of her life she'd believed it. "Okay, if you left Dad, why did he still leave us?"

Her mother jolted upright in her seat. Even Kaitlyn's eyes widened with surprise.

"Your dad never left you. Why would you say that?" her mother asked.

"Because that's what he did. He left his family to travel around the world, hardly ever coming home," Jade explained.

Jade's mother folded her arms on the table. "That's his job. He didn't leave because he took off on holidays, he left to provide for us. And as soon as a flight was done, he came back to spend time with you kids. Even when we separated, you were the first thing he came home to."

She looked toward Kaitlyn, hoping for support. But her sister only stared back with a sad expression. "Dad always tries when he's home, and he calls all the time. When we were younger, he was never gone for over two weeks at a time. And when he came home, he'd spend every day with us before he had to fly out again. Now that we're older, it's changed. He knows we have our own lives to live, but he's constantly in touch."

A knot tightened in Jade's chest. Could she have gotten it wrong all these years? Were the breaks in between his flights not as long as she'd imagined? At the time, she was only a kid, could she have exaggerated the time frame? And Kaitlyn was right. Every time he flew into Brimland Point he'd arrange for them to spend time together. He often called, but Jade didn't always answer. Was she the one who'd put the distance between them?

"You were young when we separated and such a Daddy's girl. You were his shadow, following him around everywhere. I should've known you'd take it the hardest. But you seemed so strong. I never knew you thought he left me but most importantly *you*." Her mother lifted her hands and covered her face. "I'm so sorry, Jade. I tried protecting you from the separation only to have made it worse."

Jade slid her chair closer to her mother and pulled her hands away from her face. "It's not your fault. Divorce is never easy. You did the best you could."

Tears shone from her mother's eyes. "I'm still sorry, sweetheart. If I'd known you'd been carrying this around with you all these years, I would have put things right."

"I know." Jade hugged her.

"Maybe now you can make things work with Nate?"

Jade could now hope for love and family in her life, but the only man she could picture in that role was Nate. Her heart dropped. The curse wasn't real, but Nate was leaving her anyway.

hen Jade arrived home, she found Toby sitting on her front steps. Her heart skidded to a stop. Was something wrong? Had Nate left without saying goodbye? She removed her helmet and locked it in the back compartment of her moped and rushed over to him.

"I still can't believe you ride that thing. And why yellow?" He shook his head.

She had more pressing matters to discuss than her awesome machine. "Why are you here?" Her voice trembled, and she cleared her throat. "Has Nate gone?"

Toby rose. "No, not yet."

Her shoulders slumped with relief. "Is everything okay? I don't normally find you sitting on my front steps."

She walked past him to unlock the door, and he followed her inside.

"I wanted to see how you're doing. A lot has happened these last few days."

Jade dropped onto the couch, and Toby took a seat next to her. "I'm fine." Her mouth tried lifting into a smile only for it to wobble.

Toby removed his glasses, placed them on the coffee table, and rubbed his eyes. "I tried to talk to him. But I'm not sure if what I said sank in."

Confused, Jade turned to look at him. "What did you say?" She didn't need to ask who he was talking about.

"We were at his grandmother's house. She knows he's not doing what he really wants with his life. He's living his father's dream, not his own. She knows it doesn't make him truly happy. *I* know it doesn't make him happy, so I asked him to think about letting the band go."

She took a deep breath to calm her racing heart. "And what did he say?"

His expression looked hopeful. "He said he'd think about it."

The palpitations in her chest kicked up in speed, and she had to clear her throat before asking, "He really said that?"

"Yes. And if you forget about that family curse and tell him how you feel, he might stay."

"The curse isn't real."

"What? You've been telling me for years it is."

"My mother told me it was an old tale my ancestor made up along with a bunch of others. When I told her Dad left because of the curse she realized I'd taken it too seriously and explained what really happened."

Toby's mouth fell open for a beat. "You've never spoken about that to your mother before?"

She lifted her shoulder in a half-shrug. "I guess it was easier to believe in a curse than my father leaving us because he wanted to."

"Now that you know the truth you can do something about it," Toby suggested.

A nervous sensation fluttered in her belly. "Like what?"

Toby threw his hands in the air and shook his head. Then he looked at her like she was an idiot. "What would the two of you do without me? Go tell him you love him."

Jade bit her lip. "How do you know how I—"

"Because sometimes I know you better than you know yourself. Change his mind. Nate's crazy if he walks away from you."

"I can't ask him to leave the life he's worked hard for. It's important to him," she said.

"It's making him miserable."

"What if...he doesn't..." *What if he doesn't love me?* she wanted to ask.

And like Toby read her mind, he said, "You'll never know unless you try. I can't tell you what you want to hear, but he has strong feelings for you too."

Her stomach clenched. Could she lay her heart out? What if he rejected it? But what if he gave her his too? Could she let him go without ever knowing for sure?

She bounded off the couch. "I have to find Nate."

Toby wanted Nate to think about staying, think about a life with Jade. And that's all he'd been doing, but he still hadn't come up with an answer. When he thought about walking away from her, a knot the size of a basketball slammed into his chest.

Reaching his next stop, he parked in the visitor's area. He got out of the car and walked along the pebbled path that led to a cream sandstone crypt. Dusk had fallen, and he should have felt creeped out alone in a cemetery, but lights shined over the manicured lawns and it wasn't creepy at all. In fact, it was beautiful and peaceful.

Etched in the stone above the black wrought-iron gate was the name *Miller*. Taking the key out of his pocket, he put it in the lock and the door swung open on silent hinges. It took a moment for his eyes to adjust to the dim interior. He found a light switch by the door and flicked it on. A soft, golden glow filled the room of marble and stone. Thanks to the weekly fresh flowers Fi-Fi arranged, the place smelled like a florist.

No one knew where his parents were truly buried. Fans thought they were laid to rest in a cemetery in New York. When they'd passed away, Fi-Fi couldn't bear having strangers taking photos of their graves like a tourist attraction, and she had their bodies moved to Australia and placed in her family crypt.

The names *Liam* and *Natasha* were the only names marked on the plague where they were buried. She'd kept *Harvey* off in case anyone figured out who they were. Not that anyone could get in without a key. But she didn't want to take the risk.

Nate sat on the cold floor, leaned his back against the wall, and spread his legs out in front of him, looking up at his parents' resting place. Sadness pressed heavy on his heart.

"I'm living your dream, Dad." His deep voice echoed through the room. "I've kept the Harvey name alive."

He remembered the last conversation he'd had with his father in the custom-built music studio attached to their house.

His father was playing an electric guitar, and Nate played an acoustic. They were jamming to an old Pink Floyd song, lost in the sounds they were making.

When the song ended, his father gave him a smile, and put his arm around Nate's shoulders. "You have my talent, son. You still need a lot of work, but it's getting better. Never let the Harvey name die."

At first Nate was excited by this; it was the first time his father didn't tell him he sounded terrible. "I've been working on some songs. Do you want to hear one?"

"Sure," his father said, a little distracted as he fingered the strings of his guitar.

Nate only played a few seconds when his father stopped him. "What the hell was that?"

Nate dropped his head. "It's my new song."

His father laughed harshly. "You're not playing for some pussy boy band. We're all about rock-and-roll. Not that crap."

A lump clogged in his throat, and his cheeks burned. "I like this music."

His father stared at him like he'd grown two heads. "No son of mine will play that shit. Promise me you'll forget about it and play the music men should play."

"But—"

"You'll be an embarrassment to my name. I haven't taught you how to play for you to throw it all way. Promise me."

If he didn't promise, his father would stop playing music with him. It was the only time they spent together. "I promise," he said in a small voice.

"Good, and don't let me hear that shit again." Then his father did something he'd never done before. He ruffled Nate's hair and gave him a pat on the back. "I love you, son. You're a good boy." And he left the room.

That was the last time Nate saw him.

The memory blasted through his mind and pierced his heart almost as if it had only been yesterday. He pulled air into his lungs like he couldn't breathe. All he ever wanted was for his father to love him. And when he played his music, he did. How could he stop?

And then he thought of Jade. She'd hit him like an explosion of bright, bubbly light. Making him want things he'd thought were out of reach. A normal life, his own dream...love. Because he loved Jade. And always would.

He glanced up at the wall with his parents' names. His stomach twisted into a knot. He knew what he had to do.

Chapter 28

*A*fter Toby's visit, Jade rushed to see Nate only to find he wasn't home. She knew he hadn't left yet because she could hear Dorito meowing from the other side of the door.

Back at her house, she kicked off her shoes, took her phone from her bag, and sent Nate a text asking him to come over. What she needed to say to him couldn't be done over the phone. Nerves fluttered like a flock of birds in her stomach.

She stared at the phone, waiting for a response, when a knock sounded at the door. Could it be Nate? Jumping to her feet, she took a few steadying breaths and went to answer the door.

Nate stood under the dim yellow glow of the veranda light, and her heart tripped at the sight of him. The nerves dancing around in her stomach a moment ago now took over her body.

"You were fast." Her voice shook a little.

He frowned with confusion.

"I just texted you to come over." She smiled. Then she noticed the cat cage he held. Her heart sank. This wasn't a good sign.

She gestured for him to come inside. Once in the living room, Nate put the cage on the floor and opened the latch to let Dorito out. Jade watched as the cat carefully stepped out and took a long look at his surroundings, wandering around the room until he found a dark, sheltered spot under an armchair.

If Jade took a big interest in the whereabouts of Dorito, it was because she didn't know how to say what she wanted to. Toby said Nate was thinking about staying, but obviously he'd made up his mind. And his decision didn't include Jade.

But she couldn't let it end like this, not without him knowing how she felt. It was now or never. And if she didn't tell him, she'd regret it for the rest of her life. And maybe, just maybe, once he heard her out, he'd want to stay.

"Can I get you anything? A coffee?" She had to say something. The silence was crushing.

"No, thanks. I should get going. I've got an early flight in the morning." He slid his hands into the pockets of his jeans, not looking like he was ready to leave. But not looking like he wanted to stay either.

She took a couple of steps closer to him, and with a calm voice that belied her quivering emotions, she said, "I need to tell you something."

She wanted to reach out and touch him, hold him in her arms, and let the emotions trembling through her heart pour into him. And she wanted to feel them back from him. But he stared at her with an unreadable expression.

Taking a deep breath, she wrung her hands in front of her. "All these years I've been wrong about the curse. It doesn't exist."

His eyebrows rose. "I'm glad. How did you figure it out?"

"My mother explained the story I believed in since I was a kid was an old diary written by a crazy relative. Apparently, there are dozens of stories like it. None of them true. And I guess I needed a reason for why my father left. Because why else would he leave my mother? They loved each other—or so I wanted to believe. How could he leave his family? But my mother told me *she'd* left him. I guess they weren't as in love as I thought. I've wasted years believing in that stupid curse. It was the way I dealt with the separation. My dad wasn't home often so the story *had* to be true. I should have let it go once I was old enough to understand. If I'm being honest, deep down I knew it sounded crazy—*was* crazy." She shrugged. "But I needed to believe in order to cope." She exhaled a long breath. It felt like a weight had been lifted off her chest now that the curse had released its binding hold on her. "And I'm glad I did."

He gave her a confused expression. "Why do you say that?"

"Because if I didn't believe in the curse, I could've

been in a serious relationship by now or maybe even married."

"That would be a good thing." But he frowned like it wasn't good at all.

She shook her head. "No, not a *good thing*, because then I would never have met you." His shoulders slumped, and he looked away for a moment. But she continued on anyway. "I tried using the curse as an excuse not to get close to you. Tried to shield my heart so when you left it wouldn't get broken. But it didn't work. I still fell for you."

"Jade—"

"I need to finish." She held up her hand. "I want you in my life. I can't imagine you not in it, and I'm hoping you want me in yours too. Please stay."

Rubbing his hands over his face, he then blew out a long breath. "I can't stay. The band… I need to keep it going."

She didn't miss that he didn't tell her he wanted her too. Cracks were forming in her heart. "Is that what you want? Does it make you happy?"

He scrubbed a hand on the back of his neck. "It doesn't matter if it makes me happy. It's something I have to do. I'm sorry."

"What about us? What about what we've had these last few weeks? Surely I haven't imagined the connection?"

He dropped his hands on her shoulders and stared into her eyes. Sadness clouded over his. "What I feel for you is more than I've ever felt for anyone."

Hope shot through her veins. "If the band is so important, then I'll go with you."

He let his arms fall to his sides. "I can't ask you to do that."

"You didn't. I'm offering."

"It would never work."

"You were the one to suggest it." She wrapped her arms around her middle, trying to hold herself together.

"I was wrong, I shouldn't have. My lifestyle isn't easy. Throw in the disguise and it's impossible to have a normal life. I've never been able to commit to anyone because I've had to lie about what I do for a living. But even though you know about everything, our life together would be too hard, and it would eventually make you miserable. I couldn't hurt you like that."

But he was hurting her now, the cracks in her heart growing bigger the more he spoke. "You won't even try?"

He shook his head. "You'd only end up hating me. I couldn't live with that."

God, she almost did what she promised him she wouldn't do. *I will not cry and chase after you when you leave.* But that's exactly what she wanted to do.

Barely holding it together, she nodded. Her throat was so tight she couldn't speak. She turned away, unable to watch him walk out the door.

Nate paused at his car and then kicked the tire. Dammit, he was the biggest arsehole on the planet. He'd hurt the one person he cared for the most.

He wanted to go back inside, pull her into his arms, and kiss her like there was no tomorrow. She'd probably kick him out before he had the chance. After the way he rejected her, he deserved it.

So before he could change his mind, he got into his car and drove away. It was for the best. She needed a man who could give her one hundred percent. Not someone who'd come and go whenever there was a break during touring.

Yes, it was for the best. So why did he feel like something had shot him in the chest?

Chapter 29

The phone in Nate's pocket buzzed the second he walked into his apartment in Manhattan. He dug it out and saw Toby's name lit up on the screen. Feeling too drained to talk to anyone, he wanted to let it go to voicemail. He'd just spoken to Toby two days ago at his grandmother's house. But what if it was important? What if it had something to do with Fi-Fi or Jade?

He slid his finger across the screen to answer the call. "Toby, is there a problem?"

"Yes, there's a problem. It's Jade," his friend answered.

At the mention of her name Nate's fingers tightened around the phone and his heartbeat raced. "What's wrong? Has something happened?"

"*You* happened. What the fuck did you do to her? I told you I'd kick your arse if you hurt her. And I'm tempted to get on the next plane out there to do just that." Toby's anger vibrated through the phone.

"You've seen her?"

"Yes, I've seen her. Only because I threatened to break down her door if she didn't let me in. I can't believe you fucking left her. She's a mess."

Nate sunk down on the nearest couch, placed his elbows on his knees, and dropped his head in his free hand. "She'll be okay." Give her time and she'd forget all about him.

"How the hell do you know? You broke her heart and took off before you saw the damage you did."

A cold tightness invaded his chest. "I tried not to hurt her. I explained why I had to leave. My lifestyle isn't good for a relationship."

"Then change your lifestyle. You hate it anyway," his friend spat.

"Toby, you know why—"

"Yeah, I know, you're keeping your father's memory alive. Great. But what did he do for you besides teach you how to play guitar when he had a spare five minutes once every six months? Hardly Father of the Year to hold in such high esteem. He was a shit parent. I'm sorry to say that, but you need to hear it. And you're putting him before someone who loves you and would do anything for you. Someone who handed you her heart. Someone I know you love too. But you left the best thing to ever happen in your life. And if you can't see that, then you deserve to be miserable."

With that, the phone went silent. Toby hung up.

Nate threw it at the wall, shattering it into pieces, and shoved his fingers through his hair. *What the hell does Toby know?* But Nate had told him enough about his childhood for him to understand what his life had been like.

He rose and paced the room. As a kid, Nate rarely saw his parents. And when he did, it was brief. And so, when his father told him that one time that he loved him, it was like winning the lottery.

When Jade asked him to stay, she hadn't said she loved him. But he could see it shining from her eyes. Could feel it the last time they'd made love. And that was better than winning the lottery. She'd handed him the world. And he rejected her by walking away.

It was time to stop living his life for other people—people who were never in his life enough to deserve such devotion—and do what made him happy. Be with *who* made him happy.

But before he could fly back to Australia, he needed to sort a few things out first.

Picking up the landline phone, he dialed Mike's number. When he answered, Nate said, "Get the band here ASAP. I've got news."

Jade was done crying. She'd sobbed on Toby's shoulder and on Ava, Lauren's, and her family's shoulders. But now it was time to put on her big girl panties and face the world. She'd chosen Wonder Woman today because she was fierce. Well, she'd pretend to be until it happened.

It had been three weeks since Nate left, and she'd been through hell and back. But no more. It was time to pick up the pieces. With the curse finally broken—well, it was never really true—she didn't live under the shadow of it anymore. Maybe one day she might fall in love again, but at the moment, it hurt too much for her heart to imagine.

The distance she'd put between herself and her father was closing. They'd made plans to catch up, and she no longer avoided his calls. Their relationship was slowly growing stronger.

Too many memories of Nate surrounded her here in Brimland Point, and to try to truly get over him, she needed to leave. She'd miss the place. Miss her family and friends, and Dorito too. But it was what she needed to do to help her heart heal.

A knock sounded at the door.

"I'll get it," Connor called out. Her brother was giving her a lift to the airport.

She quickly scanned the room in case she'd forgotten anything and headed toward the living room.

"What the hell are you doing here?" she heard Connor growl.

"I need to see Jade." The answering voice sent shivers down her spine and turned her knees to jelly. Steadying herself, she placed a palm on the wall and peered around it in the direction of the front door.

Connor stood with his legs braced apart and his arms crossed over his chest, blocking the doorway. "She doesn't want to see you, so get back in your car and piss off."

"I'd rather Jade tell me that." Nate stood his ground, not intimidated by her brother still dressed in his police uniform.

"You've missed your chance. She's leaving," Connor snapped.

"She's leaving? For how long?"

"Indefinitely."

"If you won't let me in, at least tell her I'm here and let her decide if she wants to speak to me or not." Was that desperation Jade heard in Nate's voice?

"I won't tell you again—"

"It's okay. Let him in." Jade stepped into the hall. She was a little worried her brother might pull out his gun and shoot Nate.

Connor gave a stern look over his shoulder. "I can have him taken off your property in minutes."

She shook her head. "I think the neighborhood has witnessed enough drama on my front lawn lately."

"Yeah, that's because of this piece of shit," Connor sneered.

"Let him in." Jade's voice shook.

Connor blew out a frustrated breath and stepped aside, peering down his nose as he let Nate enter.

For a moment Nate and Jade didn't move, only stared at each other. She drank in the sight of him like she hadn't seen him in months.

Then her attention flicked to Connor who stood like security at the door. "Can you give us a minute please?"

"I think I should stay," he said as he scowled at Nate.

"I've got this." She wasn't sure she did, but she didn't need her brother scowling at them.

When she stared him down, he huffed, "Fine, but I'll be just outside if you need me." He said this to Nate with a cruel grin on his face like he was hoping he'd have to come in and intervene.

They watched him leave and slam the door behind him.

"He's pretty protective." Nate smiled, but it didn't quite reach his eyes.

She wondered if he'd been as miserable as she'd been these past weeks. Probably not; he was the one who left. Now he was back. Why?

"He cares about me." She lifted her palms and shrugged. "Why are you here?"

Chapter 30

*J*ade was leaving town. The suitcase sitting by the door confirmed what Connor had told Nate. Thank God he made it back in time.

Nate's heart swelled as he gazed at Jade. Never had he seen anyone so beautiful. But when he looked closely, he saw that her eyes had lost the sparkle, and her face was missing her bubbly smile. He'd never forgive himself for putting the sadness in her expression. He wanted to pull her into his arms and kiss the sorrow away.

"Nate, I have a plane to catch." She shuffled her feet.

"Where are you going?"

"Tell me why you're here," she said instead of answering.

He pulled his phone from his pocket and handed it to her. "I need you to watch something."

"I don't have time for this."

"It's ready to play. Just swipe the screen."

She frowned at him and then at the phone but did what he asked.

He stepped closer, watching over her shoulder, and breathed in her sunshine and floral scent. God, he'd missed her. But he needed to stay focused.

The screen lit up, she pressed *play*, and his band, him included, filled the screen. She glanced over her shoulder at him, their lips so close it took all his self-control not to kiss her.

"What is this?" she asked.

"You'll see."

She looked at the phone again. The interviewer thanked the band for their time, made a little small talk, and got down to why they were there.

They stood in silence as they watched the clip. When the interview ended, her hand shook when she handed back the phone.

"You've quit the band?" Her voice sounded a little high-pitched.

He nodded.

"Why haven't I heard anything about this? This news is huge."

He slid his hands in his pocket; they itched to touch her, but he couldn't—not yet. Maybe never. "It's pre-recorded and airing tonight. I wanted to be the one to tell you before the news broke out."

"But the band is your way of keeping your father's memory alive."

"I realized I didn't need to dress up and play his kind of music to do it. There are other things I can do. I'm kinda going Graceland style and opening his house as a museum and displaying my parents' stuff. I've had it in storage for years and constantly had offers from people to purchase it, but I never wanted to let it go. Now I can display his stuff for the fans, my mother's fans too. Even for me when I feel the need to see it."

"Won't people wonder why you've just disappeared?"

"I'll have to make the occasional appearance. A photo now and then will get leaked to the media. But it will eventually die down, and I'll soon be forgotten."

"It's a lovely idea, but for years it's been your life." She looked skeptical.

"My father's life, not mine. He shouldn't have manipulated his young son with scraps of time and rare expressions of affection and make him promise to give up his life for something he didn't love. I have a new life now. One I hope you'll be a part of." His stomach quivered. God, he hoped he wasn't too late. "I screwed up big time. I'm sorry I walked away from you when you asked me to stay. It was the biggest and dumbest mistake of my life. You're the best thing that's ever happened to me."

Her eyes filled with tears. *Please let that be a good sign.* He risked taking hold of her hands. They trembled in his, but she didn't pull away.

"I love you, Jade. I'm pretty sure I fell for you the second you ripped off my wig and saw through my disguise. You saw past the rock star. Hell, you didn't give a fuck about him. You just saw me."

Tears spilled down her face, and he cupped her

cheeks, wiping them away with his thumbs. He rested his forehead on hers.

"I'll never walk away from you again," he promised. "You are *home*."

"What if you change your mind and miss the spotlight?" Her voice trembled.

"Not a chance. It was never what I wanted. It's *you* I want—need. And I'll never change my mind about that."

She nibbled her bottom lip and searched his eyes, then a slow smile spread across her face. "You love me?"

At seeing her smile, he wanted to sag on the floor with relief. "Yes."

A gush of air escaped her lips, like she'd been holding her breath. Then she placed her hands on his chest and pushed him away.

Shocked, he could only gape at her.

"I've been miserable for weeks!" She slapped her hands on her hips, and her eyebrows slammed together.

"I'm sorry. I've been feeling like crap too," he said.

"I'm leaving." She pointed to her bags.

His gaze flicked to the luggage sitting by the door. "I'm hoping you'll stay. Your family and friends are here. They need you here. Please don't walk away before we can try to work this out."

She frowned. "I'm booked on a six-week European tour. I'm sure they won't miss me that much."

"But Connor said…" Nate shook his head. Her brother had made it sound like she was leaving for good. But she was only going on a holiday. The tight knot in his gut loosened. "I'll go with you."

"What if I don't want you to?" She crossed her arms over her chest.

"I'm hoping you will." His heart pounded.

The smile was back, and she ran a couple steps toward him. Red curls bouncing around her head, she threw herself at him, wrapping her arms around his neck and her legs around his waist.

"Does this mean I'm forgiven?" he asked.

She planted a long, hard kiss on his lips. "You're forgiven."

Those words were like music to his ears, but there were three little words he'd give anything to hear. "Is there something you'd like to add?"

She sighed as he ran his lips along the sensitive skin on her neck. "Get your clothes off?"

"I can arrange that, but I'm thinking you might have something more important to say to me?"

Her eyes sparkled with mischief as she grinned at him. "You're hot when you look so serious."

He shifted and made to put her down.

"Okay, okay. I love you," she said, stopping him. "God, I've never said that to another man before. I've never even come close."

"Then I'm one lucky guy."

"If you kiss me, I'll make you even luckier."

He didn't mistake the invitation in her gaze. Carrying her, he moved closer to the wall and pushed her against it.

"Oh, for Christ's sake. My fucking eyes." Connor's annoyed voice boomed behind them. "You two will put me into therapy," he grumbled as he slammed the door behind him.

"Poor Connor. He's seen things no brother should." Jade made a face.

Nate laughed, but it turned into a groan when Jade tightened her grip around his waist. But he restrained himself from ripping off her clothes and taking her up against the wall.

"Jade, I mean it when I say I'm never leaving you. I love you. I'm in this for life."

Her eyes misted. "For life."

Epilogue
EIGHTEEN MONTHS LATER

*H*eavy rock music pounded all around Jade. It even vibrated up her feet and into her chest. She stared at the musicians on stage. The lead singer of Harvey's Territory was doing a good job entertaining the crowd.

Firm, strong arms wrapped around her waist, and a hard body pressed against her back. Nate's lips touched her ear, and his warm breath sent goose bumps over her skin.

"You better not flash your boobs at the lead singer to get a backstage pass." He spoke loud enough for her to hear him over the music.

She turned in his arms, putting her lips against his ear. "He's cute. I wonder if you could get his phone number for me?"

Growling, Nate nipped at her earlobe. "Over my dead body."

She laughed, then asked, "Do you miss it?"

He glanced over her shoulder at the band. "Not one bit."

And she knew he meant it. She could see no longing for what he gave up in his expression. In fact, he looked happy—at peace with his decision.

Jimmy from Sonic Sound had taken over Nate's position. He'd already accumulated a big fan base with his previous band, and they were happy to follow him. The transition had been smooth. Although Jade would always believe Nate had done a better job.

"Do you think they like it?" He nodded his head toward a bunch of kids jumping up and down and pumping the air with their fists.

Jade turned to look at the seventeen and eighteen-year-old boys and girls Nate had taken to the concert. They were students at his new music school he'd opened in Brimland Point. From playing at Jovi's Pub and teaching at Jade's school—which she was also back doing —word of mouth spread. And as soon as doors opened, all his classes had booked out. She was so proud of him. He was wonderful with kids, and they loved his lessons.

"Absolutely. You've made their day. They'll never forget it."

"I'd like to make your day." He once again nibbled at her ear. Her knees shook. If they weren't in the middle of a concert, she'd climb him like a tree.

Nate had made more than her day. He'd made her week, her month, her year. And in two months' time, he'd make her his wife.

Jade was truly, madly, crazily in love.

Acknowledgments

Firstly, I want to thank my loving family, Tom, Jaime, Ryan and Leah. They're always so encouraging and supportive and my number one fans! A special thanks to the members of the Romance Writers of Australia who always have an answer to my many questions. A huge thanks to TL Swan and her Facebook groups, Cygnet Inkers and S S Cygnets. The ladies in those groups are so encouraging and supportive. I've learned so much and gained the confidence I needed to tackle this adventure on my own. Finally, to my amazing readers. I can't tell you how much I appreciate you reading my books. It makes my day! Thank you, thank you, thank you.

About Sonia Stanizzo

Sonia Stanizzo is a contemporary romance writer living in the beautiful south coast of New South Wales, Australia with her husband and three children. When she's not dreaming up stories about couples and their road to finding love, sometimes bumpy but always a lot of fun, she can be found taking pole dancing lessons, reading and writing.

Thank you so much for reading *Trouble in Disguise*. I hope you enjoyed meeting Nate and Jade and loved them as much as I do.

 facebook.com/soniastanizzowriter
instagram.com/soniastanizzowriter

Say Hello

Visit my website to join my reader newsletter for free books, new releases and giveaways. Come and say hello on social media:
www.soniastanizzo.com
soniastanizzo@gmail.com
Facebook.com/soniastanizzowriter
Instagram.com/soniastanizzowriter
TikTok

More titles by Sonia Stanizzo

Trouble in Love Series
The Trouble with Mr. Pretty
Chasing Trouble
Acting on Love Series
Risk Taker